# False
# Relations

# Also by Michelene Wandor

## Fiction

*Guests in the Body*

*Arky Types* (with Sara Maitland)

*Tales I Tell My Mother* (with Sara Maitland, Zoë
Fairbairns, Valerie Miner and Michele Roberts)

*More Tales I Tell My Mother* (as above)

## Poetry

*Upbeat*

*Touch Papers*
(with Judith Kazantzis and Michele Roberts)

*Gardens of Eden Revisited*
(Published by Five Leaves)

## Drama

*Five Plays*

*The Wandering Jew*

*Wanted*

*Strike While the Iron is Hot* (Editor)

*Plays by Women* (Vols 1-4) (Editor)

## Non-Fiction

*Carry on, Understudies*

*Post-War British Drama: Looking Back in Gender*

*Drama Today (1970-1990)*

*The Body Politic* (Editor)

# False Relations

## Michelene Wandor

Five Leaves Publications

www.fiveleaves.co.uk

# False Relations
*by Michelene Wandor*

Published in 2004 by Five Leaves Publications,
PO Box 81, Nottingham NG5 4ER
www.fiveleaves.co.uk
(c) Michelene Wandor

Five Leaves acknowledges financial assistance
from Arts Council England

ISBN: 0 907123 201

Design and typesetting by Four Sheets Design and Print
Printed in Great Britain

## Acknowledgements

Toccata and Fugue and Via Angelica were commissioned
by BBC Radio. Earlier versions of Whose Peace, Rick, and
The Danger of Angels first appeared in *Guests in the
Body*. Whose Peace was also performed by the Royal
Shakespeare Company. Song of the Jewish Princess was
first published in *Storia 3*. Musical Chairs was first pub-
lished in *Storia 5*. Corridors of Light and Shadow was
first commissioned in dramatic form, with music, for
Radio 3. Yom Tov is also published in *Mordecai's First
Brush with Love* (ed Marion Baraitser, Loki Books).

The cover illustration, Pruning Roses, is by Anita Klein,
whose work can be seen on www.anitaklein.com
and at The Boundary Gallery in London.

# Contents

*This book is dedicated
to my sons,
Adam and Ivan*

# The Devil in
# the Cupboard

The first time I saw the devil in the cupboard was at four o'clock in the morning. I had just finished painting the flat — white walls, white doors, white ceilings. White dust covers hooded anonymously shaped piles of furniture; cardboard boxes full of books created square and oblong khaki mountains. The beds in the spare room were piled high with shapeless mounds of clothes. It was like being in a timeless world of promise.

Everything was pure. Fresh. New. Wonderful. That night I walked barefoot up the warmly varnished wooden stairs, made the bed with clean sheets, flung my clothes over a chair and got into bed naked. Cooled by the white cotton, I fell asleep, in a home that was cleansed of the clutter and turmoil of the past.

I don't know what woke me. I sat up in bed, hot, the sheet crumpled. The luminous dial on my clock said 4am. The moon was casting bright shadows through the curtainless windows. I straightened the sheet and was about to lie down again, when I noticed that one of the cupboard doors was open. I got up to close it, and, as I put my hand on the door, the devil said, "Hang on a minute."

I knew it was the devil, because I could see that he had two little protuberances, like a baby goat's horns, on his forehead. I knew it was the devil, because he had cloven hoofs neatly crossed in front of him. I knew it was the devil, because his tail was neatly wrapped round his left arm. I knew that the devil was a "he", because the evidence was unselfconsciously visible. And I knew it was the devil, because I was starkers, and not in the least self-conscious about it.

"What the hell do you want?" I asked.

"Hell is the operative word," he said.

"Have you woken me up in the middle of the night for a theological debate?" I asked.

"Sit down," he said. "I want to talk to you.

I sat on the edge of the bed. "This had better be good," I warned.

"You're unhappy," he said.

I was wide awake now. "You've got a nerve," I said. "I'm a woman of the twenty-first century. I have a rewarding job, I own my flat, I have a balcony on which I can have coffee and croissants for breakfast on Sunday. I've got wooden floors, and as many books and CDs as I want. I go to the theatre with my friends. I save money and go on exciting holidays. I've trekked in the Himalayas, tramped through the jungle of Ecuador and scaled the pyramids. I am not unhappy."

"Oh?" said the devil. "And what about love? Passion? Romance, the marriage of two minds?"

"I have lots of really good friends," I countered. "Anyway, what does the devil know about love?"

"More than anyone," he said. "And I know a love-less creature when I see one."

"Takes one to know one," I riposted — and then realised what I had said. "Ok," I sighed. "My life lacks the blessing of true love. But that doesn't mean I am unhappy."

"Wait," he said. He was out of the cupboard, and sitting beside me on the bed. "I can show you the way to true love and happiness," he said, his sharp green eyes holding mine.

"Pigs might fly," I said. "Why me?"

"I need your help," he said.

"Me, help the devil?" I laughed in disbelief.

"I am at the end of my time in limbo," he said. "I have endured the tortures of hell, and now I have to do a single good deed, and then I can be admitted to paradise."

"Why were you sent to limbo in the first place?" I asked, my curiosity whetted.

"That's another story," he said. "I'll tell you if you'll help me."

"So I'm to be it?" I asked. "I'm to be your good deed?"

"Yes," he said. "You are it."

I turned away momentarily, then, as I looked back, I saw he was standing by the cupboard again, cradling a bowl of fruit and vegetables. The scent of lemon and basil and garlic filled the air.

"I will set you three tasks," he said, "and then we shall both be free. We are both in limbo. We are both searching for true, heavenly happiness. Together we

3

can find it."

His voice drifted over me. I said nothing. I didn't need to say anything.

"Your first task is to become the greatest cook the world has ever known, the chef to end all chefs, the gourmet to crown all gourmets…"

And, reader, I did. I travelled to the mountains of Tibet and learned the secrets of spiced lentils washed in icy mountain streams. I travelled through the searing deserts of Africa, learning the cooling draughts that soothe the night-time palate. I plumbed the succulent depths of the potato latke, the infinite variety of the Turkish delight, baby carrots from French valley farms, zucchini from Italian fields. I baked and steamed and chopped and marinated, and soon I was a celebrity, famous all over the world, TV shows, guest appearances, the author of books with luscious, shiny pictures.

And then I met him. A dark, brooding man, with melting brown eyes. A painter. When he painted the fronds of the dill plant, you could smell its caressing flavour. You wanted to put your hand out to catch an over-ripe cherry before it tumbled. We fell passionately in love.

I rented out my flat and moved in to his. He was a man inspired and possessed. I cooked and he painted. I soon learned to love sitting silently in a corner of his studio as he worked, making him dark, fragrant coffee in a white swirling jug, and crumbly biscuits infused with fresh fragments of ginger. Afterwards, I crept away to the bed in the spare room, lest my breathing disturb the dreams he needed for his work.

After a year, I woke up one morning, saw my recipe books with their pages unturned, my copper pans dulled, my herb garden overgrown. I realised I no longer loved him. While he was still asleep, I dropped a kiss on his nose and left.

I moved back into my flat. My friends had watered my plants and kept the furniture free of dust. I painted everything white. Fresh. Pure. Wonderful.

On my first night there, I stretched luxuriously between freshly ironed cotton sheets, and fell into a calm, dreamless sleep.

I sat up suddenly. It was four o'clock in the morning. There was the devil, sitting at the bottom of my bed, the same sharp green eyes, the same cloven hoofs.

"Well," I said triumphantly. "That didn't work, did it?"

"Three tasks," he reminded me. "Are you ready for number two?"

I could see now that a length of shimmering blue-green silk was draped round his neck. In one hand he held a large pair of tailor's shears, and in the other a chunk of tailor's chalk.

"You," he said, "will become the greatest designer in the world. You will establish the taste of nations. You will invent colours and shapes that will astound everyone."

And, reader, I did. I dipped my batiks and silks in colours drawn from the earth and trees and plants from all over the world. I tacked and back-stitched and ruched and smocked and gathered and lined. I learned to love the silkworm and the rayon-yielding tree bark. By simply smelling and feeling a piece of wool, I could tell you from which country, region, farm and even field, its animal donor had come. I invented synthetic fabrics which transformed the lives of those in need. No-one lifted a needle before my spring and autumn designs had hit the fashion pages.

It was at a fashion show that I met him. A finely-boned face, blue eyes, long, wavy, deeply auburn hair. My sculptor. He had seen my work, and my shapes and patterns had inspired him.

We fell passionately in love. He took my real colours and shapes and transformed them into wild and mysterious sculptured forms, which captivated the art world. I loved watching him work, and he loved having me near him while he worked. I loved brewing him dark, fragrant coffee in a swirling white jug, and baking him crumbly biscuits with the zest of lemon hovering around them. I made him brightly coloured smocks to wear while he worked, and at night I crept away to the bed in the spare room, lest my breathing interrupt the dreams he needed for his work.

After a year, I woke up one morning and saw my sketch pads unopened. I saw piles of fabric gathering dust, and I knew I no longer loved him. I dropped a kiss on his nose and left.

I moved back into my flat. My friends had watered the plants and kept the furniture free from dust. I painted the walls white and revelled in their fresh purity. Wonderful.

That first night, I fell asleep immediately between the crisp, white cotton sheets. At four in the morning, I sat up suddenly. There was a sound in the room, a sweet, soaring, poignant sound.

There was the devil, sitting at the foot of my bed, his sharp green eyes looking at me as he drew a bow across a string instrument of a kind I had never seen before.

"I know what you're going to say —" he began.

"Good," I said. "Because I've had enough."

"One more task," he said, the bow drawing the most exquisite sound I had ever heard. It filled my head and ran through my veins to the tips of my toes and to the ends of my fingers. I had no power to protest any more. I knew what the task was. I knew what I had to do.

And, reader, I did. I learned to play every instrument ever made. I learned to draw any sound I wanted, from the most subtle clavichord to the largest, most resonant church organ. I trumpeted and I fluted and I drummed. I played the old and the new: the cello and the viol, the recorder and the saxophone, the racket and the euphonium. I was as content and adept on the folk instruments of South America as I was with the Indian raga tradition and the repertoires of Beethoven, Mahler and Cage.

I performed and recorded, from plainchant to freeform jazz. At one of my concerts, a man waited patiently until all the fans had dispersed. Then he came towards me, diffidently holding a sheaf of papers. He was stocky, vibrant with energy.

"I wrote this for you," he said. "I hope you have the time to look at it."

It was as if he had read my inner being, and written music designed to touch my soul and to make

7

me want to play it and touch the souls of others.

At the premiere he was modest, only taking his well-deserved bow when the audience refused to stop applauding.

We fell passionately in love. He wrote and I performed. I grew to love hearing the way a piece moves from sketch to completed form. He loved playing his work to me, and listening to my reactions. I loved writing out the parts from his scores, feeling the notes move and swirl under my pen. I loved making him dark, fragrant coffee in a white swirling jug, and shortbread biscuits covered with dark, bitter chocolate. At night I crept away to the bed in the spare room, lest my breathing disturb the dreams that brought him new melodies and harmonies.

One morning, I woke up and saw the broken strings on my instruments. I heard my piano jangle out of tune. My reeds were dry and brittle, my music dusty. I knew I no longer loved him. I dropped a kiss on his nose and left.

Back in the flat, the plants were watered and the furniture was free from dust. This time, before I painted the walls white, there was something I had to do.

When everyone else in the street was asleep, I collected all my cookery books, pots and pans and dishes, and piled them in the middle of the road. Then I took all my design books, all the brocades and lawns and linens and added them to the pile. Then, with the strength of ten, I pushed the pianos and the harps, carried the lutes and guitars and lyres, the oboes and sackbuts, and added them to the pile.

It was a dry night, and the flames quickly took hold. A warm wind blew the petals off the blood-red roses and purple clematis in front of my house, each petal catching fragrant fire as it landed in a rain of light and colour.

"Well done," said a voice behind me.

I didn't need to look round.

"True love?" I yelled, against the roar of the fire. "I've wasted the best years of my life looking for the impossible. I'm sorry if you can't make it into heaven because of me. You picked the wrong person."

"What's the problem," he asked. "You can cook, you can sew, you can play."

"That's right, I can cook, I can sew and I can play. Big deal. The perfect little housewife."

"Isn't that enough?"

"Of course it isn't enough," I shouted. "I want to paint. I want to sculpt. I want to compose."

"Well," he said, "what's stopping you?"

"What's stopping me?" I was beside myself. "What's stopping me?" I stood back from the fire, and thought for a moment.

"Nothing," I said calmly. "Nothing at all, when it comes down to it — except for true love. Of course, if I can inspire them, I can inspire myself. I might paint. I might sculpt. I might compose."

I smiled at him. It was four o'clock in the morning.

"Can you make coffee?" I asked him.

"Can I make coffee?" he said. "Is the Pope a Catholic?"

I do hope you can come to the wedding. The cupboard looks small when you first open it, but believe me, that's just an illusion. Inside, it's heaven.

# Song of the Jewish Princess

My thunderer blew in through the door, autumn leaves swirling behind him, green and brown scraps of the fading year barbed on the frayed strands of his wild woollen cloak, dry twigs pinned on his shoulders under the wide strap that held his bag, one lone leaf poised like a dancer on the brim of his hat.

Today, he who was always on time, he who always closed doors behind him, he who held himself carefully in his own space, today he was tousled, windswept, his cheeks red, his nose glowing and bulbous, his eyes wrinkled against the winter wind, his mouth taut with hurry and cold against the grin that I knew could warm his face. Well, he said, what are you all waiting for?

I hushed my body's desire to rush to him, and began to play.

*I am the original Jewish princess. The authentic article. The instrument on which the real music, according to the text, can be played. Play me. I shall sound true to you.*

It was a long day. We stopped only for wine and bread, and the bitter goats' cheese Carlos had brought with him. He worked himself and us hard, and did not talk to me, except to make points about the music. By early evening, I was shivering with tiredness and expectation.

As we all walked through the cold stone halls to the Hall of Mirrors, I huddled into my own deep blue woollen cloak, the colour of the evening summer sky. Coming in from the cold, the wave of heat from the Hall hit me full in the face. The guests already assembled there hardly noticed our arrival, and scarcely nodded an ear in our direction as we took up our place in one corner and began to play. As usual, the king and queen talked throughout, but I knew that any flaw in the performance would invoke sarcasm and complaint from either Ferdinand or Isabella the following day, and no musician was safe from their criticism.

Halfway through the evening some late guests arrived. The huge wooden doors creaked open to admit them, and the gusting wind blew out all the candles except for two — one behind me and one behind Carlos.

Momentarily the buzz of conversation died away, and in the brief pause, we played our star piece of the evening. Strings and wind and voices flashed into the dark, and between verses Carlos and I improvised on our fiddles. For the first time that day he and I looked fully at each other, our eyes so alike, green flecked with brown, flashing across the Hall, each lured by the pool of light behind the other's head. I swear that we invented fire that night.

Flame spiralled and pirouetted between our notes, held in the slim, flickering plumes of smoke. For those few moments, the chatterers were silenced. When we had finished, the ripples of music flowed into the corners of the Hall, and the assembled company applauded. Carlos nodded at me in approval and desire.

*I can pick up any instrument and bow or pluck or blow and it will speak. My mother was the same. The bow cuts deep and springy into the string, and I curve my body in reply.*

When Carlos came into my room that night, he shut the door quietly and carefully. We still did not speak until he was warm under my blue woollen cloak, and his body felt as familiar to me as my own. Isabella, was all he said. His green eyes held mine, and as we deepened into each other, our movements fitted easily, as they always had.

*Play me. I shall sound true to you.*

Later we lay, my face nuzzled into Carlos's armpit, smelling cloves and camomile, mixed with the acrid savour of satisfaction. There is something I must tell you, he said. I caught my breath. You're going back to her, I said. I knew it.

He flipped himself over so that he could look at me. It isn't that, Isabella, he said. I began to cry. Every time I see you, I said, it feels like the last time. She won't let you go. You can't leave the children. I hate goats' cheese.

He put his hand over my mouth. I licked his fingers. He whispered. He was late this morning because he had heard that soon all Jews would be banished from Spain. I am Jewish, Isabella, he said, and you know what that means. I must leave before I am killed. My wife and the children have already left. I took them to the boat this morning.

If you go, I said, I will go with you. He shook his head, and this time I put my hand over his mouth, and told him about my mother.

Never have an affair with a musician, she said. A scribe, a soldier, a goat farmer if you must, but not a musician. When I was tiny, she let me pluck the strings on her fiddle, showed me how she tightened the tension, let me hold the bow in my fat hand, and promised that one day I would be able to play as she did.

She was right about that, although she did not live to hear it. She also didn't live to see me disregard her advice about musicians. No doubt she would have smiled. My father, you see, was an itinerant musician, a man from North Africa, a Jew, a wandering minstrel who probably left behind him as many children as musical memories.

He came to our village one night, in the height of summer. My mother's husband was away in the mountains, with the goats. It was late and no-one saw him arrive. My mother gave him shelter. He played to her. The next morning he wrapped his ud, the instrument which is so like the courtly lute which every amateur plays here, and he disappeared. My mother said his fingers were like spider's webs, trailing and caressing the strings, no

14

frets to hurdle the fingers, allowing him to bend their tunes to his will. He was dark-skinned. With green eyes.

My mother told me all this the night before she died. The soldiers came — looking for "infidels". My mother was Jewish, but she thought no-one knew. She told me the story about my father, gave me her blue woollen cloak, and made me go and hide with the goats. Her charred body was flung on the ground some days later. I think about her often. I wonder how long it took for the thick earth to rot her flesh. I prefer to think about that than to wonder what the Inquisition did to her. I also worry, because I cannot remember the colour of her eyes.

*When a string is ready to snap, it plays sharper and sharper. It cries for the attention which can do it no good. My life is fraying at the edges. I begin not to sound true to myself.*

The following afternoon, two musicians, carrying instruments, strolled towards the town walls. Carlos and I also each carried a small phial of poison. His alchemist friend had assured him that whoever swallowed it would fall asleep long before the poison began to eat them away. We promised each other through our tears that we would die rather than be subjected to torture.

The soldiers on guard by the town walls laughed and applauded as we cavorted with our fiddles, mad court musicians aping their wandering minstrel brethren, a lower caste, vulgar and uncertain and despicable. So harmless and silly were we, that they

allowed us to wander through the gates and sere-
nade a flock of goats herded on a hill opposite.

*I have left my texts behind me.*

We slept in a field. Next day, lulled by the quiet of
the countryside, we were reckless. A small town,
sleepy in the early afternoon haze, suddenly came
alive with shouts and screams. Soldiers and locals
chased a small group of people, men, women and
children. An old man tripped and fell, just beyond
the entrance to the alley in which we hid. The crowd
kicked him bloody and limp. Then they hurtled past
us, knocking us aside, and when they had passed,
Carlos was no longer with me. I waited, huddled in
an abandoned house, hoping he would come. When
it was dark, I searched a little. The streets were
strewn with dead and wounded. No-one dared to
touch them. I dared not stay.

*I have had to learn how to improvise all over again.*

Memory can be kind. I remember endless roads and
fields, green streaked with brown, brown with green.
I could not eat. I felt sick all the time. My fiddle
opened doors to me, gave me beds and food. I took it
all, and more often than not gave it to the next beg-
gar I met on my way. I searched every face for the
familiar mouth, for the green eyes. I learned that
northern Italy, Mantova, Ferrara, Venezia even, were
the places to go. I hardly noticed that my periods
seemed to have stopped. The roads changed everything. In any case, the real me was somewhere else,

with a man whose hair curled over his collar, whose crooked nose could wrinkle in glee, whose eyes were like mine.

When I finally cried, my imagination flooded out of me. I bled for four days as I had never bled before. Now I knew that Carlos and his child were gone from me for ever. To the rest of the world he had never been. To me he could never be again; neither cloaked in rage not clear in love. Just misty in my music as I played.

*My text comes from the heart. Nothing can be more authentic.*

Giovanni has brown eyes. He is kind. He is good. He is my rock. He is calm and decisive and he waits for me to love him. I should love him. I am grateful to him. After all, he picked me out, a grubby, weary, wandering minstrel, travelling round Italy, playing anywhere, and he made me into the highest in the land — in the region, anyway. I am the Duchess. I am his Duchess.

Of course, no-one knows that I am Jewish. Merely that I am Spanish. I speak Italian impeccably, with a soft, sibilant accent. When I am asked when I left Spain, I say 1490; if I told them the true year, 1492, they might associate it with the expulsion of the Jews, and wonder.

Giovanni is much older than I am. His first wife died in childbirth. The son, Carlo, a wayward child, was sent to fight with Giovanni's mercenary army against the Turks. Make a man of him, they said. When he returns, he will be Giovanni's heir. So it does not matter that I do not seem able to conceive. I can make love whenever Giovanni desires, except that for me there is no love in it, merely gratitude.

I ached so much from wandering. I had to stop. This seemed the only way. Here I continue to play as I please. My musicians are the finest in the region, envied by the whole of northern Italy. I even pay them on time.

*When my strings have settled, you can play me. Then I shall sound true to you.*

And then, on a rough, blustery winter day, Carlo came home. Here, in the north, in the vast flat plain, on the river that flows to the sea, it rains and rains. Nothing is ever free of mud.

That evening there was a concert. I played in the last piece. Just as we were about to begin, the door burst open, and a young man thundered in, bringing gusting rain and leaves with him, his cloak flung over one shoulder, rough boots, a crooked nose, hair curling down to his shoulders.

I played just for him, my heart pounding, my arm quivering, my sound small and sweet. His eyes were on me the whole time, burning me in tune.

*Every text contains within it the music of a thousand others.*

Next day, Carlo came to see me. A young man, weathered, with no sign of the previous night's thunderer.

Teach me to play, he said. Teach me to play like

you. He looked at me, and in his eyes I saw Carlos again, and the baby I had never known, and something else, someone new, whose body was as familiar to me as my own, and whom I could not touch, except strictly in the line of duty, to show how to balance the instrument, to hold the bow, to flex the wrist, to find the notes.

He was an exemplary pupil at first. He rewarded my efforts by working hard and throwing himself into the music like a child. He hated being a soldier, he told me. He was not going to be a ruler. He wanted to be a wandering minstrel, to travel on the road, to live free of all ties and responsibilities. I teased him. You're too spoiled, I said. And I gave him the most fiendish musical exercise I could invent, as if that would keep him with me for longer.

*Let us play our texts to each other. Perhaps we shall sound true.*

There was nothing I can think of that precipitated the crisis. One day he blundered through the notes, careless, discordant, sullen, the bow catching strings and sullying the sound. When he finished, I exploded. Why? He flung the bow on the ground. You, he said, I cannot play to you. You create the conditions of performance. You make me feel every piece of music must be perfect, and if I fall short, I am damned.

I am your audience, I said. If you can play to me, you can play to anyone. But I can't play to you, he said. I don't know why. I just can't. Then you'll never make it on the road, I taunted. Music happens

19

because of you, not because of your audience.

But you're such a natural, he said. Who taught you? No-one, I said. I taught myself. I learned as I travelled. I learned as I played in fields and I learned as I played in courts. Above all, I learned as I got to know the instrument, until it became as familiar to me as my own body. You're the real thing, he said, the authentic article.

He said it with sadness, his shoulders dropped, his back bowed, his legs apart, his elbows on his knees, his fingers clamped together in a double fist. A lock of hair fell forward over his face. I lifted it, and one finger brushed his cheek, warm and soft. He looked up, his eyes green, just like mine.

*I am newly strung, with fine gut, translucent, springy. Play me. I dare you.*

What can I tell you. That in the moonlight, in the haven of my tower room, the room of my music, his body felt more familiar than my own. That his skin was warm where mine was cool, and mine warm where his was cool. That we fitted easily until we were the same temperature, and could not tell who was who, and he was not Carlos and he was not a baby and he was not my stepson and I did not know who he was.

You have everything you want, he said, his cheek against my breast. You have a husband who adores you. You are gifted. You are beautiful. You know nothing about me, I said. I have heard you play, he said. That is enough.

I am not what I seem, I said. I don't care, he said,

I should have married you. I cried and he kissed my face. He smelled of cloves and rosemary and permanence.

And then the door was kicked down.

*It takes only a split second to snap. Much longer to be tuned.*

Tonight I shall take poison. I shall go out into the dark. I shall cross the river by the small stone bridge that curves over the water at an angle. I shall turn right on the opposite bank and walk along by the river for a few paces, until I am opposite the tower in which Carlo and I made love.

*I am taut.*

The guards let me have my fiddle this evening. They think my husband is wrong to have his adulterous wife beheaded. I think he is wrong too; but he knows that he has no alternative at his own court. If he let me live, he would have to face me every day, and see his son in my eyes.

The guards have brought me my blue woollen cloak and the cushion on which Carlo and I lay. I shall put the cushion between me and the cold, damp stone. I shall wrap myself in my deep, blue cloak. I shall drink the poison. I shall fall asleep before it begins to tear me apart.

*I am the real thing. The first Jewish princess. The authentic instrument on which the musical text can be played. Play me. I shall sound true to you.*

21

In sunlight, the river is green. My mother's eyes were green.

# Corridors of
# Light and Shadow

The windows on the train from Verona have fluttering lace curtains. Fine white muslin, caught up in a coy waist about two thirds of the way down the curtain.

The curtains are yellow. Giallo. Giallo is also the word in Italian for a detective film.

The sun is setting as we leave the station, an old-fashioned sounding chuff-chuff train, with a whistle, which sounds like an upward sliding note played on a soprano recorder. A Renaissance soprano recorder with a wide bore, pitched at A460, a fair amount higher than our standardised modern pitch of A440. A pure, hollow sweet note, calling to the red streaks in the sky as the sun sets, as we pass the market gardens of the Veronese, the flat fields in the Po valley. Now and again a genderless silhouette bends to the ground or leads a horse towards a road.

As we approach Mantua, the street lights begin to star against the blue-grey streaks of the sky. The compartment is overheated. The curtains blow in the breeze, cool on his face. He arrives smiling in the dark. He likes arriving in the dark. He always arrives in the dark if he can.

He takes notes as he travels.

\*\*\*

*terra rossa*
*my red country*
*my red bricks*
*my red roof*

\*\*\*

She stands at the top of the campanile di San Andrea. Mantegna is buried in this church. She thinks about Mantegna every day. She is reminded of him wherever she goes. The angle of a roof against the sky, the lattice of a window, the house with the round courtyard open to the sky.

At night she often climbs to the top of the campanile to look down at the last stragglers. Old women hurrying home with bundles on their heads. Men clattering alongside their horses. Children running and shouting, a dog barking.

Tonight is unusually clear. The square is quiet. She is about to leave. A dark blur comes across the square towards the church. A shape in a dark cloak. A hat with a shimmer of silver on it in the moonlight, the sliver of the moon reflected in the curve of the hat. The figure comes towards the church steps, and then veers off to the right, to the alleyway alongside, and disappears.

***

*in the dim*
*church marble is cold*
*white*
*dim*

***

She walks through the church. The old caretaker is
waiting for her, shining his lamp to show her out,
grumbling under his breath as he waddles behind
her. She does not apologise for keeping him. He
shuffles behind, holding his lamp up to light her to
the top of the steps, then closes the church door, his
grunting cut off by the slam.

Outside, she stands for a moment, remembering
the chill dawn when the horses were brought into
the church to be blessed before the battle with the
Turks. The year escapes her. The horses' hooves
were muffled, not so much for silence, but to protect
their shoes from slipping on the smooth stone, their
harness jangling. The sound of the horses in her
mind is overtaken by a car driving across the
square, its fat tyres clanking soft and heavy on the
cobbles, displacing pockets of air. The horses strode
proudly through the air. Into and out of the church,
moving from foot to foot as the priest intoned and
the incense filled the air. Afterwards, the smell of
horse dung hovered, mixing with the holiness of
Matins.

She begins to descend the steps. The mist lies low
on the lake. She cannot see the lake from the piazza,

25

but the damp sheen of the stone speaks of warm mist, drifting and caught. The cobbles shine in the moonlight.

Her feet are cradled in soft cloth, bound over her shoes. The faint rustle of her cloak and her light, fast breathing are the only sounds that mark her. She hears a clear, light, hollow sound. She stops, a cloaked figure, who, in silhouette, looks like every statue of the Virgin Mary in every church in every city. The sound begins again, a trail of notes, ascending.

***

*at night*
*feet hurry*
*whispering in the darkness*

***

Whispering between the wheels, secret snatches of another place, another time.

I always arrive in the dark. Climbing up the slope from the water, I walk on the grass, my shoes darkening with moisture as the mist encloses them.

I walk through the city. The Castello di San Giorgio now behind me, I cross one of the many bridges. I stop in the middle of the bridge, look down along the length of water below, lined with houses, boats bobbing at the edge in the slight current. I feel mischievous. I take out my soprano, a single length of wood, carved into its fipple mouthpiece, unwrapped from its fleece, a fleece from a newborn lamb.

26

I blow a note, testing my mouth, my ear, sending the sound skimming along the water between the buildings. It is a sweet, hollow sound, a smoke ring of sound. I follow the single note with a rising scale in the Dorian mode. I tongue the notes softly, a tender "l" sound, somewhere between an articulation and a slur. The sounds are like bubbles blown from a soap pipe, the faint echo overtones bowing back to me from the dark silence. I wait for a moment. No-one stirs. Not even a dog barks. I am where I want to be.

***

*my sounds*
*are wrapped*
*in bright, cerise silk*

***

She turns as the sound comes to an end, and crosses swiftly and softly to the Piazza Sordello, slips in past the guard at one of the side gates, and finds her way to bed. Tonight the Duke has not waited for her, and is snoring when she eases through the half open door. Around her the portraits of his family blink and tut at her lateness, laughing behind their hands at her damp hair and her out-of-breath. She throws an angry glance at them and they freeze back onto the walls. She drops her cloak onto the floor, slips her shoes off and slides under the heavy wool covers to join him. His arms snake round her waist and they sleep.

*** 

*a red rose*
*scarcely full-budded*
*in a centimetre of water*
*not able to peer*
*over the glass's rim*

***

Weaving in among the dark streets, I find a doorway.
Huddled in my cloak, the night offers gentle
reminders as the church bells renew themselves
throughout the night.

***

*the bells*
*can never lie*

***

In the distance, in dreams, from somewhere in the
Piazza Sordello comes a tune, soft, sweet and carrying. It is called "Pastime with Good Companye", and
it comes from another country.

***

*the slightest fall from grace*
*is seen*
*like a rose*
*beheaded*

***

The following morning she is up before the Duke wakes. As she picks up her crumpled cloak from the floor, he turns over in bed. She does not kiss him.

The following morning the bells summon the faithful and the unfaithful to church. The new arrival watches them from the doorway of the merchant's house, then he moves across, along the cloisters into the Piazza Sordello. Diagonally opposite to the Palazzo Ducale is the Bar Gonzaga. A young man in a white apron wipes the tables clean from the night, and gestures to a clean, dry white chair. Sit. Prego.

***

She is on her way home with a basket piled high with plums from the market. She always crosses the Piazza Sordello, a short cut back to the ghetto, though no-one calls it that. Yet or any more.

She sees him stirring his coffee, holding a cake in his other hand. She stops by his table. He looks up. These are simple gestures.

Excuse me, she says.

He smiles.

*my eyes are telescopes*
*I can see for miles*
*and round corners*

A scooter races bouncing across the cobbles, a harsh, edgy mechanical wasp whine. It drowns his reply

29

and her response to his reply. She points at the recorder.

Was that you playing last night?

He is not sure what lies behind her question, so he does not respond.

In the Piazza Sordello. No-one plays in the Piazza Sordello at night. What was it?

A tune, he says. Why doesn't anyone play in the Piazza Sordello at night?

The palace guards don't like buskers, she says. May I join you?

He gestures towards a chair and she sits.

I'm not a busker, he says. I am a musician.

Oh dear. If you had been a busker, I would have given you some money.

You can buy me another coffee, he says.

She puts her basket down and waves to the waiter. He nods and goes back into the bar.

So, she says. You are a musician. You're not Italian. But your accent is very good.

Thank you, he says. The coffees arrive fast. Grazie. Prego. She puts money on the tray.

Are you hungry, she asks?

No. But I will be, he says.

She reaches into the basket for a handful of plums and puts them on the fleece near the recorder.

There. That's instead of money. Plums for a musician.

Do you often do this, he asks, taking a plum, and wiping the bloom of dust on his cloak.

Oh, no, she says. I never talk to strangers. But then, you do not seem to be a stranger.

It's the first time someone has bought me

breakfast, he says. And the first time I have played in a strange country at night.

What's your name, she asks.

Henry. Yours?

Isabella. Enrico. I like it.

Where do you come from?

Another country. Far away.

She laughs. That sounds like a line. A convenient excuse for irresponsibility.

Perhaps. But it is also true.

Why are you here? How long are you staying.

The square is filling with people, men in twos talking and gesturing, women hurrying children to school. He looks round, leans forward and speaks softly.

I am here on a mission.

She laughs again. A musician on a mission? He nods.

Will you tell me?

It is a secret.

Oh, of course. She nods, playing along. And women are not very good at keeping secrets.

Exactly. He leans back in his chair.

But, she says, stirring the froth lightly on the top of her cup, I am also a politician. And I too have a secret.

Will you tell me?

Only when I am sure I can trust you, says Isabella.

Henry opens his arms wide. But I am far from home. Whom could I tell?

Isabella shrugs and opens her arms wide. You might get very drunk one night and tell someone here, in Mantua. That would be worse than telling someone you know.

He nods. Very well. We shall each keep our secrets.

Until we know one another better, she adds. They hold out their hands at the same moment and shake.

\*\*\*

*walk under a bridge*
*hear your voice echo*
*as you look up*
*and shout*

\*\*\*

She puts her hand to her forehead. Of course. I know your secret. He waits. You are the king of England.

He smiles, with modesty. How could you tell?

The tune. Last night. I have heard it. We had an English lutenist who played here last year. He played music which he said was written by the king of England. Pastime with Good Companye. Written by Henry the Eighth.

Did you like the song, he asked?

Oh, we laughed. He translated the words for us. Bucolic, extravagant, boastful, we thought. Not as subtle or as wistful as our own Bacchic conventions.

Now it is his turn to look enlightened. He leans forward. I know who you are, he says.

Isabella Gonzaga, formerly Isabella d'Este, now Marchesa di Mantua. Patroness of the arts, music in particular.

\*\*\*

*under the bridge*
*high metal rings*
*to which criminals were hauled*
*and left*
*hanging*

\*\*\*

A bicycle clatters loudly across the cobbles. Its wire-framed basket bobs on the metal, rhythmic, regular. In the basket are beige and purple onions, small bunches of lavender. A purple onion bounces out of the basket and rolls under the table. The boy on the bicycle is oblivious, now standing up to exert more pressure on the pedals, speeding away across the square.

Why doesn't everyone recognise you, he asks. This is a small city.

I am wearing ordinary clothes, says Isabella. I look like all the other women. Would you like to see the city?

Now?

Of course.

But —

Even a marchesa must have a day off.

She stoops to pick up the onion and then stands up, picks up the basket of plums. She puts the onion among the plums. You can hardly tell the difference, she says.

I'll find you some red silk, she says. For the recorder. You can line the fleece with it.

33

\*\*\*

*there are rules*
*for everything*

\*\*\*

They walk down the left hand side of the Piazza Sordello. She points up at the delicate crenellations above them. This is the Castiglione house, she says. Baldassar looks down on me, frowning, because I explode his codes of conduct. He watches the castle opposite from his window. His eyes are like telescopes. He has written a book. He takes the rules of rhetoric and turns them inside out. He doesn't mean a word he writes, but it goes down well as a stick with which to beat those who try to step out of line. The politicians love it. The politicians also love Machiavelli.

\*\*\*

*an enclosed grille*
*overhangs the street*
*criminals burn*
*in the heat of the day*

\*\*\*

They walk under a bridge over a road. They stop and look up. Isabella hoots softly and the echo returns to them.

34

Those small metal rings in the arch, she says, are rings through which transgressors are hauled and from which they are left hanging. Sometimes alive and sometimes dead.

Transgressors, comments Henry. Do you mean criminals?

I don't know whether I mean criminals, replies Isabella. The Palazzo Ducale first, I think, she adds.

*\*\**

*vaulted ceilings*
*now painted white*
*a map engraved in marble*
*two layers of red brick on the wall*
*one old, one new*

*\*\**

Into the ante-room: diamonds and lozenges painted on the wooden ceiling. Were you born here, asks Henry.

No. I was born in Ferrara. I came here when I was seventeen.

My age when I became king, says Henry.

Isabella smiles. We have so much in common.

I think you are older than I am, says Henry.

Yes, says Isabella. Does it matter?

Nothing matters, says Henry, not when the king of England walks with the Marchesa di Mantua.

*Non fa niente*, says Isabella. What does that mean, asks Henry.

*the sly suggestion of a lance*
*fine lines faded*
*on the wall*
*the coy implication*
*of a battlefield*

Isabella leads him down uneven stone steps, worn into oval shallowness. Pisanello, she says. The man who did not come from Pisa, just as I do not come from Mantua. But here he joined my country and yours. Look. The knights from Arthur's round table on the walls, high on the wall — look, up there, can you see — emblems of the English royal livery entwined with our Gonzaga marigolds.

The colour of your hair, murmurs Henry, his face close to her head.

Isabella moves away from him, turns and smiles. The English do not have a reputation for being romantics, she says.

I am on holiday, he smiles. On holiday everyone is romantic.

***

*a world on a wall*
*an old world on an old wall*

***

There is the eagle, beautiful and predatory, she says, walking on. Pisanello and his birds and animals, each feather perfect, his fine lines now faded on the

36

wall. The drawings have been ignored. We only have the suggestion of a shield, the tip of a lance, the coy implication of a battlefield.

When was this painted, he asks.

Many years ago. The early fourteen hundreds, I think. Our world will survive on our walls, when all the furniture and tapestries have gone.

The Marchesa knows her history.

I know my husband's history. It is my job.

\*\*\*

*layer upon layer of the world*
*frescoes on blue and gold*
*it is too soon for history*

\*\*\*

Isabella takes Henry by the hand and leads him through a series of corridors, up and down stairs, and eventually through a small door. The room is dim, blinds down over the windows.

\*\*\*

*terra rossa*
*my red country*
*my red bricks*
*my red roof*

\*\*\*

This is the Camera degli Sposi, she says. The room of the married couple.

La Camera Picta. He adds to the information.

Your accent is really excellent, she says.

His eyes accustom to the gloom. By the window opposite is a large bed, covers rumpled.

All cultivated Englishmen know a little Italian, Henry says.

Isabella does not reply. She draws him towards the bed and they sit. She kisses him, her right hand cradling his cheek as she does, nuzzling and nibbling, until their mouths have met their centre in each other.

\*\*\*

*the blinds are drawn*
*it is to protect the paintings from the light*
*it is to allow us to sleep*
*for as long as possible*

\*\*\*

We will leave the blinds closed, she says. The sun will wake us when it is high in the sky. As they lie back on the bed, she says, the Camera Picta. The painted room. It was finished the year I was born. Look. That little boy. The taller of the two. That is my husband, Francesco.

Henry is kissing her, and the two are loosening each others' clothes. Your husband, asks Henry.

He died last year, says Isabella. Above us is the sky. Naked putti everywhere. With butterfly wings on their backs. Be careful, because if you anger the putti, one of them may drop an apple on your head.

Henry kisses her neck, licks round the shape of

her face. I am not frightened of the putti. I am not frightened of much.

Really, says Isabella, her lips lightly nipping his fingers, the soft pouch below his thumb, the tip of each finger in turn.

I am a soldier and a hunter. I am a musician. I am not a politician. I prefer to do, rather than to think. I have learned to leave fear in my bedroom. Whose room are we in now, he asks, as his fingers find her soft, damp centre and Isabella's legs gently move apart to receive him.

There is a moment's calm silence as they join each other. Then, as they begin to move in rhythm, Isabella replies: last night I slept here.

***

*cassetoni*
*box shaped spaces in the ceiling*
*inlaid with paint*
*the muses placed safely in them*
*like the head of a red rose*
*a false ceiling*
*trompe l'oeil*

***

They lie clasped, their hearts beating fast, slightly out of rhythm with one another, their panting gradually stilled.

In another room, whispers Isabella, there are horses on the ceiling. As you cross the room and look up, they change direction. And in another room there is a zodiac ceiling, where the sky spills down

39

over the walls and you must find the door back into the world. Come. We must go.

She moves gently from below him, onto the floor, her clothes tidied. He follows, slowly, saying nothing. She kisses him on the head, ruffles his hair.

Just before they leave the room, he looks back, around it, at the bed, the window.

Will you be here again tonight, he asks.

No, she says. Tonight I sleep in my own bed.

\*\*\*

*strike someone blind*
*then make them see*
*this is magic*
*this is a conversion*

\*\*\*

They walk swiftly through one room after another. Along a long gallery shaped room, a Hall of Mirrors, their feet clicking on the marble floor. In the middle of the room, they stop. Here, she says, here you can play.

He unwraps the soprano, the innocuous wooden stick with eight holes in it, seven for the fingers and one for the thumb, the slightly curved, oblong aperture in the mouthpiece, the fipple which nestles below where the upper lip rests. It is in his mouth, his lips hold the mouthpiece so no air can escape, but gently, lovingly. As he blows, the fingers take up their position, ready to lift and settle with their deep-rooted memory. A single sound, a note, an A floats out, round, around the edges of the room and back.

A long note followed by a stream of decoration as the melodic line dances to its next strong stress flows out into the room. When he stops playing, before he has reached the end of the phrase, the reverberations tumble over one another in rippling discords before the sound dies away. T'Andernaken, he and the whispering echoes chase the notes to the walls' edges.

*\*\**

*floating in the sky*
*looking for the doorway*

*\*\**

From outside the hall a woman's voice, deep, cracking over the break, filters through. She spells out slowly and portentously a list of names: Federico Gonzaga, Carlo Federico, Ludovico, Isabella Gonzaga, Lucrezia Borgia... the names echo away from the hall. Henry looks at Isabella. My aunt, she whispers. Her husband, my uncle died last year, and she won't believe he is gone. She thinks he has lost his memory and cannot remember his name. She walks the palace rooms all day, calling out names in the hope that he will recognise his own and call back to her.

Henry has begun playing again, almost before Isabella has stopped speaking. He leads her out through the door, into the large ante-chamber beyond. He looks up as he plays. At the four corners of the ceiling are four carved black heads, looking down, lordly and foreign.

\*\*\*

*black and silver*
*her dress*
*Isabella's dress*
*ruched sleeves*
*black, silver and gold*
*her dress*

\*\*\*

We don't know where she sleeps, Isabella says. Or even whether she has time to sleep.

Henry lowers the recorder. Perhaps she is the ghost, not her husband, he says.

Isabella smiles. Perhaps we are the ghosts, she says. Let me take you to my rooms, she adds. My studiolo. My grotta. They are in the Castello di San Giorgio.

\*\*\*

*the grotta*
*is more private*
*than the studiolo*

\*\*\*

Henry wraps the recorder in the fleece as they walk.

You know your way round, he says.

It is my palace, says Isabella. But it is very easy even for me to get lost. It is more like a village than a palace, anyway.

If we get lost, says Henry, do you think anyone will notice that the king of England and the Marchesa di Mantua are missing?

*\*\**

*a grotta is a cave*
*a retreat*

*\*\**

They are in a stone passageway. Henry comments as they walk, as if Isabella is the visitor. Isabella tucks her hand in his, as if he is her husband.

*\*\**

*private*
*narrow*
*discreet*

*\*\**

A vaulted ceiling, says Henry.

According to my own design, says Isabella.

Blue and gold.

My name. Isabela. With one "l". A soft, tongued consonant.

The heavens shining around us. We are the stars in our own sky.

My motto, my device. *Nec spe, nec metu*. Neither

43

hope nor fear.

I love you, Isabella with one "l".

Musical instruments painted on the wooden panels. Viol. Lute. Keyboard.

I neither fear nor hope. I love you, Isabella.

You love my palace, I think. I hope you might love me. I fear that I might love you.

This number, asks Henry. Twenty-seven?

A pun, says Isabella. *Vinti sei*. Twenty-seven. My enemies are vanquished. Your Italian is not quite perfect. Do you have enemies?

Henry does not answer directly. What is this design?

My music, says Isabella. Blue and gold squares. Lines. Horizontal and vertical. My music.

But there are no notes, says Henry. Just rests. Silences.

Isabella answers: My music is in between the silences. My music is the silences.

Henry bursts into involuntary laughter. You Italians. You are so full of romantic rubbish.

Isabella withdraws her hand. Don't you ever hope? Don't you ever fear?

I am a king, says Henry. If I want something, I take it. Sooner or later. Give me your hand again. Mine is getting cold.

\*\*\*

*a grotta is a cave*
*a retreat*
*private, narrow, discreet*
*a corridor*
*more private than the studiolo*

44

*a place where you must stoop to peer out at the river*
*where the music huddles on the walls*
*and in the centre of each box of sound*
*Isabella's secret gardens*
*Isabella's grotta*

\*\*\*

As midday approaches, they leave the cool of the palazzo's walls, cross the Piazza Sordello again, turn right past the Piazza Herbe, past the rotunda, the round church set down in the lowest corner of the piazza. Briefly they walk inside, staring up at a shaft of light stabbing down through a narrow slit. Isabella holds her arms out, her body now in the shape of a cross.

I feel I can hold the church in my arms, she says.

I build my own churches, says Henry. If the church will not give me what I want, then I will build my own.

Isabella puts her arm round his waist. For now, she says, we can worship each other.

He places his forefinger on her lips. Blasphemy, he whispers. She opens her mouth, sucks the finger, tastes the smell of woodsmoke and garlic, then quickly, neatly, nips the tip with her teeth, then runs her tongue over to smooth away the brief hurt.

I need my finger for my music, he says, as they walk back out of the church and up the steps into the main part of the piazza.

I know she says, rubbing her cheek against his arm.

***

*crenellations*
*like almond shavings*
*surprising the taste buds*

***

They sit at the back of the small restaurant, savouring bowls of risotto, steeped in the juices of some meat that once cantered over the cobbles. Outside, church bells sing to each other, light, overlapping, jangling and discordant.

*La prima donna del mondo*, says Isabella, toasting Henry with her glass of red wine.

Henry dribbles olive oil over the rough white bread, torn with his fingers from the loaf.

A man comes into the restaurant, a bright red woollen cloak flung over his left shoulder. In his left hand a violin. He stands by the door. He tunes the strings, fast, so fast that it sounds as though he is tuning all four strings at once. He plays a series of chords, the ground bass line for Ruggiero. The first phrase: G major, C major, D major, G major. The second phrase: G major, F major, C major, D major. Third phrase: D major, C major D major. Fourth and final phrase: G major (first inversion), C major, C major (first inversion), D major, G major.

Henry looks up at him, his eyes flashing, his attention rivetted. Others at the tables look up. The chords begin again, this time semi-concealed, hidden, peeping out from behind runs of improvisations on the top string, rooted at crucial harmonic

46

moments in a chord stroked across the whole of the instrument. Gradually the eaters return to their tables, to their companions, as the music sidles and flirts with the air and renewed chatter joins it.

When he has finished, the musician walks round the tables, bowing and collecting. He comes to their table. Henry holds his hands out in a gesture, as if to say that he has no money. Isabella pulls open a small bag, tied at the neck with a blue silk cord, empties the bag on the table and a coin rolls down onto the floor. The man picks it up, bows and moves on to the next table.

After lunch, says Isabella, we will walk along the river.

***

*swim, my darling*
*whisper in the water*

***

High on the grass bank, they walk in the lowering afternoon sun. Their silhouettes accompany them on the grass below, their shadow heads touching the edge of the water. Henry picks up a stone and throws it into the calm surface.

***

*a stone in the water*
*skim across the calm sheen*
*waiting for*

*the shadow of grass on your back*
*nothing is as light as a son.*

***

They continue to walk, not touching.

Your wife, asks Isabella.

In England, says Henry. I don't want to talk about my wife.

They walk again, silent, not touching.

Church bells do not lie, says Isabella. You can never forget your wife.

I would like an Italian recorder, says Henry. For my birthday.

I may not know you on your birthday, replies Isabella.

Then I would like it as soon as possible.

A king always gets what he wants?

This island, says Henry, of all places in the world, this is the city in which I could make my home. Perhaps I shall never go back to England.

You can walk round this city in less than a day, says Isabella. You can take eternity to paint its walls. You could find a new home. Will anyone miss you?

***

*terra rossa*
*small red bricks*
*sand coloured walls*

***

48

Will anyone miss you, she asks again.

Betrothed at twelve, says Henry. My bride, five years older. I need a son.

I was betrothed at five, says Isabella. I loved my husband. Of course I loved my husband.

\*\*\*

*Perche ne la forma sta il tuto*
*non fa niente*

\*\*\*

They are crossing a small bridge. Ahead of them is a fat, squat, elegant building.

This, says Isabella, is the Palazzo Te. My son Federico commissioned Giulio Romano — the painter, not the musician. This is his palace of pleasure. No-one can see in.

\*\*\*

*what's in a name*
*a fountain*
*frozen in summer*
*needs no explanation*

\*\*\*

They are within silent shapes of stone, rooms peopled on walls and ceilings.

The salamander licks everywhere, says Henry.

In the flames, over the walls, says Isabella.

I want a son, says Henry.

Look how Apollo drives his chariot across the ceiling, says Isabella. Apollo leans forward. He wears a short skirt. He wears nothing underneath.

Isabella is very close to Henry now, her hands busy beneath his clothes.

A naked cupid flies between two trees. I need a son, says Henry.

Isabella says, come, lie down with me. I have had all my children, Henry. I am older than you.

I will be your salamander, says Henry. Jove seduces Olimpia, while Venus and Mars bathe naked among the putti. I will lick you everywhere.

Isabella is moving above Henry. I am a horse, she says, stepping proudly out of its frame, my hooves balanced on an invisible ledge. Nothing is what it seems here.

\*\*\*

*green and silver leaves*
*on a eucalyptus bush*
*a secret place*
*has no space*
*for windows*

\*\*\*

As Isabella and Henry are reborn, angels and camels and elephants pass, a man wrestles with a serpent, a swan makes love to a man in a lake, tame tigers gallop with baby centaurs, and after the banquet, the salamander licks the plates clean.

\*\*\*

*a swan makes love to a man*
*angels sing from neat*
*manuscript books*
*a wool gatherer reclines*
*white hair flowing*
*from every orifice*
*water like wool*

\*\*\*

By the time they leave the Palazzo Te, it is darkening. They walk back across the bridge, along the straight street where Mantegna's house opens to a circular sky. The house is dark, Mantegna gone, his memory clinging to the round walls in the courtyard.

If I were really the king of England, says Henry, my mission would be to find an authority who could free me from my wife so that I could marry again and have a son.

If I were really Isabella d'Este, Marchesa di Mantua, musician, patron of the arts, a widow whose son rules, I would run away from the city with a musician who carries a magic instrument in a white fleece.

Would you give him a son?

Of course I would give him a son. And a horse, and any musical instrument he wanted.

You are very kind, says Henry. I am not kind. Kindness is weakness. I must be strong at all times.

And yet you still don't have what you want. You still have no son.

I am the king of England. I can invent anything I

want. Did you really love your husband?

Yes, I loved him. But I knew for a very long time that he loved others. I became ruthless in my own right. Then I stopped loving him. I miss my husband, even though I know he did not love me.

Because I need a son more than anything, I do not have a chance to discover whom I love.

Then you have not come here to find a son. You have come here to find someone to love. Isabella sneaks her hand into his, caresses his open palm with hers.

Men can only father sons, she says, because women have given birth to daughters. I have had all my children. I can have no more. I can only offer you love.

Are you saying that beauty of form is everything, asks Henry.

If you were going to stay here in Mantua, says Isabella, we would have a marvellous time discovering each other, debating philosophy and aesthetics.

Playing music and finding new instruments, adds Henry.

Yes, says Isabella. But you cannot stay, because the world is not a very nice place, and if you are the king of England, there is nowhere you can hide. Neither hope nor fear, and leave me.

And if I am not the king of England, asks Henry.

Then you must play your soprano recorder until you find the salamander.

Isabella removes her hand and puts it into her breast. She draws out a piece of bright red cerise silk, warm from her body. Henry puts out his hand to take it, but she draws back slightly.

Promise me that you will wrap the recorder in

this silk. It will smell of ginger and violets. When you play it, wax candles will flicker in your eyes.

Isabella gives Henry the silk. He holds it to his face and then puts it in his cloak, against his breast.

One day, he says, when I am travelling back this way, I will ask for you at the court. Isabela with one "l".

One day, she says, I will find a painting of the king of England, and see whether it is in your likeness.

\*\*\*

*the clouds fringe the sky*
*an eagle nestles under a parasol*

\*\*\*

Ahead of them the water glints in the shy moon.

I came on the train, says Henry, but I will go back on the water.

He walks down to the boat and his shadow melts into its shape.

\*\*\*

*terra rossa*

\*\*\*

On the other side, he hitches a ride from a passing scooter. As they speed along the night road, they pass a cemetery, where the stones blink with names: Norsa, Finzi, Rossi, Contini.

***

*la terra mia*

***

In Mantua, Isabella goes home to her father's house. It is Friday and she is late. Her mother scolds her for missing the synagogue service.

In the palace the Duke prepares for bed, hoping the Jewish girl will come to him tonight.

In her house in the ghetto, Isabella lays her borrowed name in a cupboard, wrapped in a newborn lamb's fleece.

In the Palazzo Te, Apollo whips his chariot into a frenzy while the salamander licks the ceiling into shape.

# The Danger
of Angels

*(or Sex According to Vivaldi)*

When the sun strikes the water on a clear, clean day, you can see sudden light; sudden flashes of light. Flashes of light which you can almost hear. The flash of an octave, one note answering, echoing the other, from a higher, playful place, a spark of recognition flashing between the two. You can see figures of light, pyramids and hills and columns of arpeggios and chords, you can see semi-quavers rippling out from the octave, you can see light flashing in intervals of a dazzling major second, a minor third, a perfect fifth.

Antonio used to say that if there really was a God, then God must have invented the octave by seeing what happened when the sun struck the water and was reflected back unto itself. That would be on the fourth day of Creation, when the sun and moon were created. The ripples, the waves sent out by the water, flashing in sparks and semi-circles of light, the ripples must be the scales and arpeggios, pursuing the same sequence of patterns, over and over again, in different combinations, permutations and oh, isn't it all beautiful?

Well, sometimes. If I believe in God — and I'm not at all sure that I do — but if there is a God and a heaven, then I imagine its streets will be paved with water, and music will rise like steam in the sunlight. Like Venice. The Venice of marble and water, voices and music. The Venice of everyone else's romantic dreams.

***

Antonio is crying. Deep, wracking sobs. In bed. We are making love for the very first time and he is crying. It is all wrong. It's the woman who is supposed to be overcome with sadness. It's the woman who is supposed to be shattered at the loss of something or other, some non-existent innocence, some important moment of transition.

Here we are, holding each other, and he is crying. I am sure I must have done something wrong, after all these months, both of us pretending that what passes between us is only music, me sitting in the orchestra, watching you as you conduct, your eyes passing over me as they pass over everyone else, and there, behind every accidental, every arching phrase, we have been touching each other, touching and touching. And now, I must have done something wrong. Crying and laughing, and moving in a quiet pulse until we slip into sleep together.

***

When we give concerts at the Pieta, there is always a metal grille between us and our audience. It is considered improper for the secular gentlemen of the chapel to catch even the slightest glimpse of one of the girls, even though it is considered perfectly proper for them to listen to us play and sing. How strange. I can think of nothing more likely to inflame the imagination of young men and women than the most beautiful voices and sounds in the world, performed by invisible beings. The danger of angels is as nothing to the music we made.

The night Antonio and I made love for the first time was the night of a difficult concert. Through the bars of the grille I could see a man's hand, tap-tapping on his knee. A grey woollen knee. At first I thought he was enjoying the music, and that he must be tapping his hand in time to the rhythm, the beat. And then I realised that he wasn't, he couldn't, he couldn't hear where one beat ended and the next began, and I couldn't screen him out of my sight. My eyes kept straying to the sight of his hand — tap tap tap a chipped and flaking tap    the fingers    tap tap tap    soft and white and fat    tap tap refined    tap    polished nails    tap tap    beating and beating some rhythm which refused to allow the real rhythm through, and I can feel the wrongness tap tapping its way into my brain and I am sure that I am in the presence of the devil and that he will drag me into his dark, pulse-less world and destroy me, and finally, just before my entry in the Largo, I am saved by the music. I have been in deadly combat with the devil, and I have won.

After the concert Antonio congratulated me on my performance, and we made love for the first time.

***

From my window I can see the outer wall of the orphanage. Down there, just by the hospital wing, there is a part of the wall with an iron grate set into it, low down in the stone, reaching to the ground. Between the edge of the grate and the paving stone underneath, there is a smooth, curved hollow in the stone. There is just enough room to lay a new-born baby in this stone hollow, so that it can be slid under the grate, to the other side of the wall, into the cloister.

Every morning one of the Sisters used to go down to the grate, to see if a baby had been left there. Sometimes you could hear the baby crying. The babies were always taken in and looked after in the hospital wing, on the far side of the building, so that their crying shouldn't disturb the older girls, I suppose. No-one ever knew where the babies came from. No-one asked. The children of poor, devout people, perhaps, the children of prostitutes and foundlings, love-children; such an odd phrase.

***

I was fourteen when I arrived here. Fourteen and furious. Betrothed at fourteen, not delighted about it like my friend Isabella, oh, no, not collecting shoes in anticipation of my marriage, like Isabella, one for each year of her life, fourteen pairs, decorated with gold and silver lace, with tiny blue flowers and scarlet bows. Not delicate and good and obedient and always pretty and smiling, like Isabella, not liking the young man chosen for me by my father, a convenient arrangement between fellow bankers and a glass of Chianti to celebrate. I refuse to look at this dull, spotty boy; I don't want to know him and I will not marry someone I don't know. Kicking and screaming and tears and tantrums and here I am, thrown into prison, to learn, says my father, the meaning of devotion and obedience; to come to my senses.

I came to my senses.

*\*\**

If you walk through Venice on a summer night, past the open windows, the candles, the light, the music, everyone is singing and playing and dancing in the big houses, in the palazzi. I could play the violin when I arrived here. I could play the notes, that is. Not the music. Here I had no choice. There was music everywhere all the time. I liked the speed of sound under my fingers. Antonio wrote for me. People called me a virtuosa. People called him a virtuoso. It isn't a word I understand. The sound comes from deep within you, it is something in your being speaking through your fingers.

The first time I heard Antonio play, I recognised something. And I knew then that I was not in prison, that I had been set free from prison, that I had come to my senses.

People nicknamed Antonio the Red Priest. It was the colour of his hair, of course, but also his incredible passion. I used to hold my arm under his head at night, for fear the heat of his hair, the dark and flame and burning colour, should burn the pillow, singe the initials I had so carefully embroidered on the fine silk.

*　*　*

Antonio did not really want to become a priest. He wanted to play his violin. He had a million sounds in his head. He must write them down. His father tells him that he will find it easier to earn his living as a musician if he becomes a priest. This was Monteverdi's downfall, his father says. He insisted on marrying and having children, and this limited his career. Monteverdi would have been even more successful if he had written music as part of the duties of a priest who plays to celebrate the Divine Spirit.

Antonio takes holy orders. He celebrates Mass for a year. He has to raise his voice to sing in the Mass. When he sings with his own, human, voice, he breathes in and in, he doesn't seem to have enough air for the long phrases, he gasps and gasps and an iron band comes down across his head, over his eyes, and another heavy iron band closes itself round his chest, and his mouth is open and gasping and he cannot let go so that the air and the music can come out. His arms fall to his sides and his shoulders hunch and he staggers away from the altar and into the dark and the silence and the cool of the sacristy, and he falls onto a wooden bench and supports the intolerance of his heavy body on his hand. Gradually his shoulders fall and his jaw relaxes and in the quiet the iron bands release and he lets the air float out of him and away and the roaring in his ears settles and in its place comes a melody, a chord, notes running freely, and now, energised, he finds a quill and a piece of paper and he writes and writes until the music is caught and resting in black and white. Antonio no longer takes Mass. But it is too late to halt the rumour that he is careless of his religious duties.

Of course, Antonio's father was right. How else, but as a priest, could he have such opportunities of music. How else, but as a priest, could he have come to work in the Pieta, among the nuns and the girls, how else would I have met him, how else made music for and with him, how else could he have given me my music.

***

At the back of the building, jutting onto a small canal, dark, where no sunlight can creep into the crevices, there are the store-rooms. There the silence is dark and haunts the ears.

Me. Huge, like a whale, beached. Sister Teresa, a pink oleander flower in her hair. I am in pain. I am in agony. I shatter the silence. I sip wine and water between my agonies.

Antonio sits in the corner, hunched, among the oranges, the smoked hams, the onions and the garlic. His red hair glows. His head turns to and fro,

61

just as it does when his body sways with the movements of his arms as he plays the violin, to and fro,
and a sharp pain builds in me and I cry out and he
leaps up and runs, runs out of the room, away, away,
and the pain suddenly stops short, cut off by his
going and instead I cry because he has abandoned
me in my great need. Teresa holds me as I sob, wipes
my forehead, kisses me and strokes my hair, holds
me as the next pain touches my centre.

As I open my mouth to let the pain out, it is
accompanied by a sound of great and true beauty,
and Antonio is again there, now at my side, he and
his violin improvising to the rhythms of my labour,
to the sway and swell of the stardust in the room
and the harvest of food in the corner, the scent of
oranges and onions and the thick white wax of the
candles, and my body follows a music I have learned
somewhere else, and then there is someone else
sharing our music: Anna. Then her music takes over
from ours and she sucks at my breast straight away
and we are all silent together.

Teresa told the other nuns that she found the
baby that morning, in the hollow stone, under the
grate in the wall.

We had no choice. Some other women also have
no choice, and they wrap their babies tightly and
throw them, weighted with stones, into the dank
back-street canals of the city.

*\*\**

Antonio in rehearsal shouts, is sarcastic, is loud and
angry, is cold and sarcastic, can't you hear, can't you

land on the centre of the note, I want perfection and you will give it to me. Afterwards I call him an arrogant bastard, I say you can't have perfection without imperfection, you know that the centre of the note and the perfect harmonic sound only exist in relation to imperfect sound and discord, and what is this stupid word perfection anyway?

Who are you to tell me what is pure? Don't you know that you only want the pure because you know it is possible to misread a note, to know that one person is capable of not listening to another, that good intentions are not enough? No, no, no, his face fiery red, his nails bitten down to the quick, flat against the tips of his white fingers, no, no, no, don't you see, the whole point, the whole struggle is against inaccuracy, against imperfection, the whole point is to be absolutely in the right place at the right time.

But I don't want to hear about the right person at the right time. I see my daughter at a distance. I watch her laugh, I hear her play and sing, and I say nothing to her and she doesn't know who I am, and I have not sung or played a note since she was born and don't you dare talk to me about the right place at the right time.

Antonio and I did not make love again after Anna was born. We loved, as ever, with complete devotion, we slept in the same bed. But we never touched in the same way.

*** 

After Anna was born, I had a great desire to leave the Pieta. But where would I have gone? I did not want to leave Antonio. I did not want to be out of sight of my daughter.

Sometimes I sneaked out at night, wearing a dark cloak, carrying a basket, so that people in the streets think I'm a nurse hurrying to tend the sick, a whore hurrying to a rendezvous. I wander for hours sometimes, in the silence of sewage and the lives shouting down from back street windows. I make the journey between silence and music regularly outside the stone walls which contain me during the day.

Antonio finally left Venice for good. We had always travelled, all over Europe, and especially to Amsterdam, to his music publisher there. Dutch music printing was far in advance of its Venetian counterpart, with a clearer script, much more suitable for the shapes of Antonio's music. Anyway, Antonio was older, perhaps a little tired of Venice's insatiable demands for new music, going out of fashion, perhaps, in favour of the newer composers.

I nursed him when he was ill. I wrote the music for him when he was tired. Often I knew what was in his mind, and would finish something he had started.

I never signed my name to it. Why should I? It's your music. Alright, perhaps some of it is mine, and don't shout at me, you know it brings on your asthma. I will not sign my damn name, damn you, I will not take over where you left off, this is not my music and I would not be writing it if it were not for you. I will not play my violin, I will not go away and compose something and then play it to you. Who is going to listen to anything an unknown woman composes? Where are the women priests, the *maestre di coro*, the *maestre di musica,* need I bloody go on?

He is silent. No, he says calmly. Don't go on. Just sing to me, play to me as you used to. I swear at him and run out of the room, so that he should not see my tears.

***

Antonio died last year. Somewhere unknown. Buried somewhere, in a pauper's grave, with no name on it.

***

I have not seen Venice for seven years. Water on stone; caged nightingales singing in the little shops by the bridges, wax candles in the cathedrals, building marble shadows.

It was raining when Antonio was buried. The rain drifted through my head, sinking into the earth. A funeral hymn, soft and light, not at all sacred, water on earth on stone. I have played the music in my head all through the long solitary journey back here to the Pieta. In my old room I have written down the melody. I am singing it to myself.

***

Anna is fourteen now.

She is very dark, like me. She has a patrician nose, with a sort of bump in the middle, a wonder-

65

fully arrogant profile. She pitches herself perfectly into incessant activity; never still. She is the most beautiful thing in Venice. They tell her she is a virtuosa. She laughs at them. She laughs and laughs, in a fiery sort of way, and she sings and plays and laughs with a voice I have carried inside me.

I am going to tell her who she is.

Antonio left no will.

# False Relations

**False relation**: A contradiction between two notes of the same chord, or in different parts of adjacent chords.
(*The New Grove Dictionary of Music and Musicians*, edited by Stanley Sadie, Volume 6, pp 374-375)

\*\*\*

## ONE

The Duke held the paper up close to his eyes and scanned the list of names. In the silence, the tension was as thick as the evening mist hovering over the lake outside the window. The Duke lowered the piece of paper, and spoke. Claudio Monteverdi, he said. There was another silence. In such a homely space there was no need for formality. The decision had been quick, inevitable. There was only one man for the job. The gathering was over. Everyone simply left the Camera Picta, their cloaks rustling through the narrow door. The Duke remained alone, the paper still in his hand.

\*\*\*

*We sit, huddled in our cloaks, shielded from the night cold by the palace wall. Claudio puts some more wood on the fire. The brazier glows. We are old men, arguing about dates.*

*1605, he says. That's when Vincenzo first mentioned Orfeo.*

*No, it must have been 1606.*

*I'm sure it was 1605. Winter.*

*Every misty evening in Mantua feels like winter, even when it's in the middle of summer.*

*Work backwards from the performance. 1607.*

*Yes, 1607.*

*We agree on that, at least. The first performance of "Orfeo" was in 1607.*

*That's what it says in the documents. 1606, I say, was the first time I was exempt from wearing the badge. I remember going from your house to mine, at night, without the tell-tale badge. The Duke asked you to write Orfeo in 1606.*

*Commanded, you mean.*

\*\*\*

I have never been in the Camera Picta, the Sala degli Sposi. So my description of it comes secondhand, or more accurately something like third or fourth, or even tenth hand. My image of it is built up of different things described to me by palace servants, from occasional references from the Duke himself, from a lutenist who had played there once. Like me, Claudio never saw the room.

68

*We laugh. Claudio passes me the bottle. The Tuscan red, harvested from the fields near Siena, given to us by Leone, dries on our tongues, inspires our palates.*

***

Actually, the exact date no longer matters. We build the Camera Picta, memory by memory, the colours softening and fading slightly, the shutters closed, to prevent the colours from fading any more.

We are agreed that the room is probably empty now. No furniture. The chair on which the Duke sat probably consigned either to the fire after the plague, or transported to a palace somewhere in France, or even England, sold to King Charles 1, of England, sold to finance an impossible war.

Wherever you look in the Camera Picta, history is on the move. Information, gossip, status, travel, succession, everything is there. The occulus in the centre of the ceiling opens the room up to a circular luminous blue sky and clouds. A woman looks over the edge, a black servant in a striped headdress beside her, watchful. The naked *putti* have climbed over the edge of the occulus, ready to fly down into the room, their genitals peering down at us, their chubby legs still with rolls of baby fat around the thighs.

***

*A century before we were born, I say.*

*Mantegna worked here between 1465 and 1474, says Claudio.*

*I toast him. I thought you were lousy at dates?*

*The dates are painted somewhere in the room. Someone told me. I remembered. I don't know. I bet you can't remember what day you were born, says Claudio.*

\*\*\*

Above the door into the room, is a painted wooden banner, supported by more naked *putti*, their soft, firm genitals held before them, round and cuddly, their little globe stomachs still with the puff of youth. Their faces show signs of physical effort, slave labour, you might say, as they hold up the device. One has his hands above his head, his face looking to one side, as if to say, I am tired, how much longer do I have to stand here and hold things up?

\*\*\*

*Of course not, I say. I knew nothing about time when I was born.*

*For centuries, slurs Monteverdi, until they grow up and old and their mortal frame rots and crumbles. Those damn putti will be there for ever, barring acts of God and marauding Emperors.*

\*\*\*

I point out that one *putto* is already sitting on the ground, taking a short break before he changes position with one of the others. What if they all escape, to run outside and play, stealing cloaks to cover their fat naked bodies, what if they run away and the square of wood topples into the room?

On two walls, the one framing the door and the wall at right angles to its left (if you stand with your back to the door), are the cartoons. Scenes revealed behind painted curtains which have been drawn back. The ruling Gonzaga family, their children, servants and animals. A scene within a scene, set in an airy landscape, an open landscape with no fogs or mists, just as the occulus reveals its clear blue and white, with no grey clouds.

History is frozen, on the move.

*** 

*Who were they kidding, says Claudio.*
*Themselves and everyone else, I say. Just like us.*

***

In the distance is a wonderful, white, walled city.

***

*The city of Rome, says Claudio.*
*The holy city of Jerusalem, I say. Mantegna hadn't been to Rome.*
*You haven't been to Jerusalem.*
*Alright. Let's just call it the city of heaven.*

71

*Claudio nods and spits out the husk of a salted melon seed.*

*It falls on the cobbles, its black and white striped claws shiny in the ash.*

\*\*\*

Ludovico, the second Marquis of Mantua (not yet a Duke), his wife Barbara, two children, one of whom, Francesco, was later to marry Isabella d'Este —

\*\*\*

*Claudio and I raise our glasses to toast the tyrannical patroness of the arts.*

\*\*\*

There is Mantegna himself, sneaking in a shadowy self-portrait on a painted pillar, his carved head framed with painted carved leaves, like a woodsprite peering out of the fabric of the room within a room.

\*\*\*

*Mantegna. Mantua. The sounds are made for each other, I say.*

*You should have been a poet.*

*No. I would never have been allowed to write for the court.*

*You weren't allowed to write for the court.*

*We laugh.*

*The brazier glows. Our hands are warm.*

## TWO

A portrait. Everyone believes it is a portrait of
Claudio Monteverdi, major composer at the court of
the Gonzaga Dukes, friend of Salamone Rossi,
minor composer, Jew at the court of the Gonzaga
Dukes. There are some people who will believe that
this story, the story I am telling, is also really a portrait of Claudio Monteverdi.

A portrait is only ever an image of what it seems.
Here the graven image of a young man is of a dark
face, swarthy shadows on his cheeks. A long nose,
full lips, the mouth open, about to expand into a full
grin, the eyes crinkling round the edges. But I don't
smile, because I am looking at you, my eyes simul-
taneously focussing and slightly abstracted, because
I am watching you and listening to myself. This is
not a portrait of Claudio Monteverdi.

In the picture, my left hand is fingering a C (Ut)
Major chord in second position on the bass viola da
gamba. My third finger is on the C on the G string,
my middle finger on the E on the C string, my first
finger is on the G on the E string, barre across onto
the C on the A string. My right hand hovers over the
finger board, about to pluck the chord. The fingers
of my right hand are concealed behind a square
wooden stand which holds a sheet of music on which
are a fuzzy stave and some musical notes. The music
is smudged and difficult to read. An ink bottle and a
quill testify to my composing skills. On the wall
behind me is a violin with a decorated finger board

73

and a bow crossing its strings. My clothes are those of a minor sixteenth-century courtier. On my head is some kind of dark covering. Around my mouth is dark shadow, a moustache rising to meet the edges of my nostrils.

The picture was discovered in Cremona, and Monteverdi was born in Cremona. That is why everyone assumes it is of him. There are two other definitively identified paintings of him, as an ageing and then as an old man, gaunt, with a beard. However, without further evidence, it cannot be assumed that this picture is of him. On the contrary, it is clearly the portrait of a Jew with a viol. A Jewish musician transgressing by playing instrumental music in the synagogue.

There are few enough facts about Claudio's life. There are even fewer about me. We have more in common. Artusi took issue with Claudio's compositional decisions in the early 1600s; I too was challenged by the rabbis. I repeat: there are few facts about me. We must all beware of the histories we are fed. That is why we are here, huddled over the warmth of a small fire, and that is why when dawn breaks we shall be gone, leaving only some black and grey ashes, warm with their own history.

\*\*\*

*Claudio dozes, leaning against the edge of the door-way. I pull his cloak round him. He stirs, pats my hand and smiles, his eyes still shut.*

\*\*\*

## THREE

I think I first met Monteverdi at the party to celebrate my book, my first, in 1589. A small volume of
short two-voice vocal pieces. Italian words. Michele
Norsa paid for its publication, and he must have
invited Leone da Modena. Talented young musician,
you must meet him, Azariah's son, a talented boy,
etc etc. Leone had to have a finger in everything. He
must have brought Claudio.

***

*Bullshit. Claudio wakes himself with a snort. The
first time we met, he says, poking me in the upper
arm with a forefinger to emphasise every word, was
across a crowded Sala dello Specchio, the Sala della
Musica on a Friday evening.*

*So you're still throwing my lack of religion in my
face? I ask. Don't poke me in the arm. It hurts.*

*It's to remind you to respect your elders and betters.*

*Bullshit. We're musical equals.*

*He bursts out laughing. Musical equals? What
blasphemous nonsense! His laughter turns into a
cough.*

*There you are, I say, you shouldn't put your
youngers and betters down.*

*Bloody damp, he says.*

***

The synagogue was at the top of Michele's house, in
the attic. Michele's attic was a peaceful and joyous

place, with paintings of birds and flowers tracing the elegance of the walls, matching the holy books which we all learned to decorate with illuminated letters in the long grey winter afternoons of the Po valley. None of those books survived.

I had left my bass viol in the attic after the *Shabbat* service, and I took Claudio up to show him the instrument. I unwrapped the bass from its Turkish tapestry rug, and showed him the leaves I had carved round the scroll — a touch Claudio said was vulgar at first. He ate his words when he heard the sound I could draw from the instrument with the bow.

\*\*\*

*Bullshit, mutters Claudio, settling more comfortably. You should learn some new expletives, I advise.*

\*\*\*

Claudio unwrapped his violin from its stained linen cocoon, and we began to improvise. I played the bass line, and he the violin. Claudio's violin was warm from where it rested against his chest, the bow springy and light. My viol was warm where my legs held its ribs. We exchanged instruments, and Claudio twirled it round in his hands before he rested it between his calves, and bounced some exploratory scales from its strings. Ruggiero, Bergamasca, Passamezzo Antico. We danced round the chord patterns. His bowing style was taut, nervy, agile, mine fuller, more focussed. A perfect match.

When they called us down to play for the dancing, we began spontaneously, alternating phrases in a series of fanfares on the opening chord of the first piece, with runs of four fast notes (semi-quavers, you would say now) to the martial, dotted, slower notes (crotchets, you would say now). This was greeted with laughter, applause, and then the dancing began. You will find this moment repeated in two pieces of music: the opening of "Orfeo", and the opening of the "Vespers" of 1610. The same fanfare does double service, for secular and sacred purposes — a mix which we found was one of our many shared practices.

When everyone left that night, I fell asleep quickly. My dreams were invaded by fast, swirling notes, in equal and unequal numbers, notes we had carelessly flung into the air, which had disappeared on tiny ripples of sound out into the damp night. In the morning I wrote down as much as I could remember.

***

*How could I not remember the first time we met?*

*Claudio shakes his head. Wishful thinking. That wasn't me.*

*I throw an olive at him. It hits his cloak and bounces off onto the ground. The glance of oil deepens into a stain.*

*Anyway, he says, I had four books of music published before I was twenty. You had only one.*

*Not bad for a little yid, though.*

*Not bad for a little yid.*

77

## FOUR

Within a couple of years Claudio was employed as a string player by Duke Vincenzo, and much later came the Duke's decision to ask Claudio Monteverdi to write a *dramma per musica*, a musical and dramatic entertainment. The fable of Orfeo. Commissioned — commanded in 1606. Orfeo, *favola in musica.*

***

*You have no proof.*
   *I remember being exempted that year from wearing the badge. 1606.*
   *Anyway, the exact date doesn't matter.*

***

I remember the excitement. Arriving, instruments wrapped in cloth, strings going out of tune because of the damp, expanding near the fire, contracting near the windows. Singers coughing and sipping wine to lubricate their throats (at least, that is always their excuse!). I called everyone to order by playing a chordal flourish on my violin, and an elaborate, arpeggiated figure ending with a long trill, which outrageously stretched the cadence.

***

*I'm getting bored, says Claudio.*

*You can't be bored. I am about to make my first confession.*

*Jews don't go to confession, slurs Claudio.*

*Jews are free to confess to anyone at any time, I counter.*

*Alright, then. What?*

\*\*\*

Back first to 1595. Claudio is already working at the court. A handful of musicians are summoned to accompany the Duke to battle.

\*\*\*

*I was ill, remembers Claudio. A streaming nose and eyes, non-stop sneezing. Damp, steamy, damp, foetid Mantua.*

\*\*\*

Claudio has flu. In his room, a bundle is packed, ready for the Duke's military journey. I can't even remember what the battle was. But I was relieved that as a Jew there was no chance of being summoned to go. Claudio is desperate. Not only must he work the hot line to God in the middle of battle, but the Duke expects him to compose new music. Matins, compline, vespers, you name it. God on the run, is how Claudio describes it.

\*\*\*

*You were grateful to me then. Remember? I say.*

*Claudio sings a rising scale. I respond with another rising scale in echo, a third higher. Then we sing together, in thirds, the music which became the violin parts from the "Deposuit" movement from the Magnificat at the end of the Vespers — the one known as the "1610".*

*This is my confession, I say. I dreamed all of that.*

*What. Claudio states the word, does not inflect a question.*

*My confession, I say. I dreamed that duet, I wrote it down the morning after I met you, after we improvised in Michele's house. I gave it to you. It belonged to you as well as to me.*

*Claudio begins to laugh. And the violins punctuating the Sonata sopra Sancta Maria?*

*One of my intermedi from the Purim play the Jewish troupe performed at carnival, I say.*

*Claudio reaches for the bottle again. We toast each other, he with the bottle in his hand, I with a clenched fist.*

*No-one will ever know the difference, he says.*

***

That's how it really was.

The Vespers of 1610, originally a collection of disparate movements written at different times for different occasions, has its own history.

I wrote the music for the movements which used texts from the Psalms, Claudio set the texts with the Catholic texts. There is a secret clue to this, in my Songs of Solomon. I set the Hebrew text of Psalm

80

126, and Claudio set the Latin text of Psalm 127. I set Psalm 121, and Claudio set Psalm 122. You will find, that with some careful juggling, the Hebrew will fit instead of the Latin, and vice versa. Many of the so-called Vespers movements were tried out with simplified forces in our synagogue — the Latin texts were replaced with Hebrew, where necessary. Everything was sung on Friday, on *Shabbat*, and often again on Sunday. The Gonzaga never knew. No-one ever knew. The Vespers of 1610 by Claudio Monteverdi.

I have never been jealous, because I know the truth, and Claudio is my friend.

***

*We had so much in common, I say, my hand held out for the bottle.*

*Why the past tense, asks Claudio?*

***

We both set Petrarch's "Zeffiro Torna". We both set "Parlo, misero o taccio". Claudio's setting of the latter is for three voices, and his opening phrases derive from music he heard when he came to synagogue on *Shabbat* with me, his head covered, his eyes drinking in the sounds. This experience also survives in "Duo Seraphim", the exquisite cantorial exchange between two tenor voices, in phrases first heard between Leone and Michele, as they sang their dialogue between rabbi and chazan.

Claudio and I had so much in common; we Jews had so much in common with Catholic musicians: no real distinction between sacred and secular music. It was all music and it was all words. The same tunes for sacred and erotic madrigals, the same music for Hebrew and Italian texts.

\*\*\*

*Domine ad adiuvandum me festina, Gloria Patri et Filio et Spiritui Sancto. Sicut erat in principio, et nunc et semper et in secula seculorum. Claudio intones, the "s"s slurring into giggles.*

*Sicut reminds me of Succot, I say, secula seculorum reminds me of dor va dor — generation unto generation. Do we really have anything in common, I ask Claudio?*

*Not*
*much, he burps.*
*We drink to that.*

\*\*\*

1610 is also the year in which Duke Vincenzo resumes discussion with the Jews about the ghetto, discussions which had first begun in the early 1600s, during the pogroms, when seven Jews were hung by their feet in the square in front of the cathedral, their families banished from the city. The early 1600s, when Judit Franchetta was burned as a witch for supposedly casting spells over a nun, who had been a Jewish convert to Christianity.

Jews do not go to confession. We may forget, but we never forgive.

# FIVE

The Duke's decision was announced in the Camera Picta. Our decisions were hatched in whispers, in the Room of Mirrors. On Friday evenings, I slipped across the road after our services ushering in the Sabbath, treading silently across the cobbles, round corners into the Piazza Sordello, along the cloistered walkway which kept the worst of the night damp away, and in through a side door, through the palace, up the stairs and into the Hall of Mirrors, for the evening's entertainment.

This is not the Hall of Mirrors which visitors see now, lavish with painting and reflections, and with a resonant, bell-like acoustic. This was a smaller room above it, a hot, feverish, exciting room where new things were heard in the land.

I dreamed once that I was standing in the centre of the second, later, larger, Hall of Mirrors. Chairs were sparsely placed round the edge of the hall, with red tasselled ropes across the arms of the chairs, ensuring that no-one would sit on them.

I walked round the hall, and came to a stop in the middle of the room, took out a soprano recorder, blew some notes, and while they were still coursing round the room and returning to me, I began to play a steady line, the decorated line of T'Andernaken, supposedly written by Henry V111, although everyone knew he could not write music, or even improvise very well. But when you are a king, the history books will say that you can do everything brilliantly.

I woke from this dream with more notes coursing round my mind, with a dialogue between two full, swooping sounds, calling to one another across a crowded hall, reminding me again of the decorated fanfare which Claudio and I improvised when we first met.

*** 

*Dialogo detta la Viena.*
  *Sonata sopra l'Aria Sancta Maria.*
  *Duo Seraphim.*

*** 

I slip into the Hall of Mirrors, joining the heat of sweat and wine, sit by the door, listening to the other musicians as the courtiers chatter, their clothes receiving, absorbing and hiding the ringing music, secreted to be shaken out later, in erotic private. Claudio comes to join me, needing the freshness of the draught across his face, ruddy with wine and effort, his jacket soaked with sweat at the back.

Here we whisper.

*** 

*I can see lights in front of my eyes, says Claudio.*
  *Candles. Flickering candles.*
  *I can see flickering candles at the corners of my eyes. My head aches.*
  *Slip out, I say. I'll play for the songs. Go to bed. Close your eyes.*

84

*I can't. He wants another bloody madrigal. He wants music for Mass. He wants —*

\*\*\*

I put my hand over Claudio's mouth.

\*\*\*

*I have finished the fanfare, I tell him. For the opening of the opera. If it works well, you can reuse it for something else.*

*He looks quizzical, his eyes focussing on me with difficulty.*

*I send him home and play in his place. Jew, Catholic, what does it matter as long as you love the music. Next morning I bring him the new music, without words.*

\*\*\*

He adds words praising Father, Son and Holy Ghost. The words slip into place alongside my notes. We sing, I in Latin, he in Hebrew. We correct one another's pronunciation.

\*\*\*

## SIX

Back in the Camera Picta, the Sala degli Sposi, the paintings show events from over a century ago. Ludovico has received a letter asking him to go to

Milan. The court gathers to hear the news. Elsewhere Ludovico stands near his horse, with some pugnacious dogs nearby, one with his back towards us, his balls thrust towards us.

Two boys, one of whom is Francesco, later to marry Isabella d'Este. The motto written on the wooden panel held by the *putti* above the door reads:

"For the most renowned Ludovico, second marquis of Mantua, a very good prince of unabated faith, and Barbara, his most renowned wife, incomparable glory of women; their Andrea Mantegna of Padua made this modest work in their honour, the year, 1474."

By this Mantegna meant no more than Claudio and I meant by our sycophantic bowing and scraping on paper to those to whom we dedicated our works. Those who provide opportunity and money for works of art like to be thanked in some permanent form. Patronage, security of employment and hope for payment are the spurs behind these motifs, not respect or adoration. Mantegna did not believe Ludovico and his wife were either good or glorious, and neither did he believe that his own work was modest. He knew it was great and exceptional and witty.

\*\*\*

*The brazier is humming down. The glow sinks deep into the metal. Claudio and I shiver a little. We look at each other.*

\*\*\*

Claudio was dismissed by the new Duke in 1612. When he accepted a job in Venice in 1613, he left a box of letters and music with me. Too much to carry. Too much history. On the way to Venice, his carriage was stopped and robbed. At least the letters and papers were safe with me.

When I left Mantua for Venice, in 1628, driven out by the new conquerors, whose anti-semitism knew no bounds, I carried the box with me to Venice.

In the Venice ghetto we were able to set up a musical Academy. Leone da Modena organised the singing, set up debates about the function of music in religious worship. We called it The Accademia degli Impediti, in Hebrew, Bezochrenu et Zion, taken from Psalm 137, By the Rivers of Babylon, a setting for one of my own Songs.

Zion = Mantua.

\*\*\*

This evening we walked round the old ghetto in Mantua. From its western boundary along the market square, near the commune building, the Palazzo della Ragione. The main gate was there, leading from the ghetto market in Piazza dell Aglio to the main market, the Piazza Erbe. To the north, the ghetto bordered on the Monte de Pieta and the church of S. Salvatore near the Dottrina Christiana street. There were another three large gates and three small ones. The four large gates led to main streets and the three small ones to alleyways.

\*\*\*

*That's eight gates altogether, says Claudio, I only remember six.*

*Even about this we argue.*

\*\*\*

As we walked, the last light of the sun disappeared behind the lake. The cobbles gradually acquired a slick of wet, not from rain, but from the thick evening mist which descends so fast over the city of Mantua. Finally, we brought our wine, our porchetta, our bread and our olives to this spot, beneath one of the walls of the Palazzo Ducale, at the edge of the old ghetto, where Claudio and my worlds met.

Here we have sat, all evening, warming our hands by the brazier, eating, drinking and remembering. When I arrived in Venice, Claudio insisted that I should keep the box of papers. He didn't even want to be reminded of what was in there. Until now.

Between us now stands an empty box. Its contents, letters, music, the paper stained with myriad unidentified liquids, sometimes torn, sometimes scribbled on, has burned well on top of the charcoal.

\*\*\*

*Claudio coughs. Deep, gravelly.*
*I look at him with concern.*
*It is damp. We should go back.*

\*\*\*

We have been travelling for days now, first to Cremona, where he was born, now to Mantua. The year is 1643.

Claudio insisted on bringing the box back to the city he loved and hated. As usual, I am in disguise for my friend. I have removed the patch of orange cloth which marks me as a Jew. We are cloaked presences in the city of Mantua, and soon we will row back across the lake, and return to Venice.

Claudio stirs the fire. A piece of paper, caught at the edge, flares. Then it settles, first into white flakes, then into black, and finally into the dust of ashes.

\*\*\*

**False Relation**... One consistent qualification makes false relations acceptable: the falsely related voices or parts are nevertheless melodically coherent in themselves. (*The New Grove Dictionary of Music and Musicians*, edited by Stanley Sadie, Volume 6, pp 374-375)

# Toccata and Fugue

My mother called me Isabella —

*Isabella*

— after a sixteenth-century Italian princess, whom she read about in a women's magazine.

*Isabella d'Este*

When I was little, I used to make up stories about my former life as an Italian princess —

*Ferrara*

— at court, surrounded by painters, poets, musicians, and as many biscuits as I could eat.

*Isabella d'Este, di Ferrara*

Perhaps that was why I became an actress. It seemed so easy to imagine being someone else, living at another time, when passions were high, when love and loyalty and drama were the stuff of everyday life, even at a time and in a country very different from my own. Of course, I only imagined the exotic hedonism; the dangers of the plague, let alone the common cold, did not enter my fantasy world.

*Betrothed to Francesco when I was five years old*

I became interested in the life of Isabella d'Este, who went from Ferrara to become the Duchess of Mantua at the turn of the sixteenth century.

*Francesco was fourteen*

She wrote thousands of letters; not surprising at a time when there was no telephone, no fax, no e-mail. I don't much like writing letters but I love receiving them.

*My wedding —*

So when Lucy wrote to me, saying she was an actress, and wanted to interview me about my experiences as a leading lady over four decades, of course I was delighted.

*I rode through the city in a chariot draped with cloth of gold.*

Lucy swept through the door, a mass of dark hair curling over her shoulders. From her temples streaked plaits coloured red, orange and gold, making her head look like a sunburst.

*The streets were hung with heavy brocades and festooned with garlands of flowers. Special entertainments — plays, music, street games — were composed for the occasion, which lasted for a week.*

We clicked immediately. Lucy had done her research well, read all my reviews and interviews, and, what is more, knew her Shakespeare. Her curiosity and intelligence tickled my pride and my memory, and rekindled the passion and enthusiasm I felt for the great roles — Lady Macbeth, Gertrude, Cleopatra, Ophelia, Juliet, and, the high point of my career, my performance of Hamlet, which provoked controversy and the wrath of male reviewers.

This was the real purpose of Lucy's visit. She too wanted to play Hamlet. When I asked why, she answered — "Well, for a man who is supposed to have had difficulty making up his mind, he seems very sure of himself. And it's a bloody meaty part."

"Good for you," I said. "And if you like, I'll play Claudius to your Hamlet."

We laughed and parted, arranging lunch later in the week.

*The morning after our wedding night, Francesco went out hunting before I was even awake.*

Over dinner, I enthused to Frank about Lucy's visit. I was amazed, I said, at the way someone so young, without any apparent need for, or experience of feminism, had such an understanding of the struggles women of my generation had had to make a serious mark in theatre. "And such enthusiasm," I said. "I

93

think I'll ring my agent tomorrow. See if anything's come in."

*I spent the day alone, eating marzipan cakes.*

Frank looked up from his tagliatelle. "Good," he said sharply. "Perhaps you can salvage the part you turned down last week."

"I've told you," I answered, just as sharply, "I am tired of being offered eccentric cameos in soap operas. I won't do them."

"If you really wanted to work," said Frank, scraping his chair and getting up, "you'd take anything. I would."

"I'm not you," I snapped.

"No," he said. "You're not. I'm going upstairs to work."

It was a conversation we'd had dozens of times.

*This early experience set the pattern for our married life. I learned fast. Someone had to run the city when my husband was away, either at war or at pleasure. I discovered a taste for government, and a taste for art.*

As I got older, the jobs fell away —

*I collected delicately tinted Murano glass from Venice —*

Whereas successful male actors went from strength to strength in their middle years —

*— amber rosaries and ivory crucifixes —*

— there were far fewer roles for an actress to "grow into" —

*— crystal mirrors, lutes and viols of ebony and ivory —*

All that seemed left were eccentric old lady parts in inferior soap operas, and after doing a few of those, I realised that if I didn't stop, that was to be my fate. Not wanting to be typecast for the rest of my career, I turned them down.

*I learned to sing to my own accompaniment on the lute.*

I haven't worked for three years. Frank says I'm lazy. He earns enough to support us both; but he enjoyed basking in the glory of my performing successes. As a scientist, he feels art is far more superior to his own work in computing. At any rate, that's what he says.

*They say my voice charms the stones. I have the magic of Orpheus.*

Frank also says that if I can't work, I must be clinically depressed and I need treatment.

*They call me la prima donna del mondo.*

Of course, I have often pointed out that Frank, now one of the managing directors of a large computing firm, can have no idea about the insecurities of the freelance artistic world — that the emotional satisfaction you get or don't get from playing a particular part becomes an issue. It isn't merely a matter of money —

*— the first lady in the world —*

— but he just laughs. Basically, he believes that I have not been ambitious enough, not made enough effort on my own behalf. This, of course, makes me angry, which proves, of course, that I am emotionally unstable, which makes Frank go even more stony, and makes me get even angrier, which makes — well, you get the point, I think.

*Our marriage may have been arranged —*

Our arguments go something like this: just as you've reached the peak of your career, mine has hit a crisis point. Gender difference. Rubbish, he replies, he who has always been perceptive to the critiques of feminism, he who has been at the forefront of an equal opportunities policy in his firm. Rubbish, he replies, you're just not trying hard enough.

*— but I love Francesco and he loves me*

The following morning, Frank disappeared at seven, before I got up. He would be late back. A meeting after work. Where? A bank in the city. Don't worry about supper.

*I organised entertainments at the palace.*

Lucy and I met at the National Gallery for lunch. It felt as if we'd been friends for years, despite the gap in our ages.

*The back of the stage was hung with cloth of gold.*

We talked non-stop. About the way the feminist movement had affected my life and career — about her own career. Very little had changed; it was still harder for young actresses to be taken seriously, and she filled in the gaps between jobs with office temping. Boring, but it paid the rent.

*The roof was hung with sky blue cloth —*

My children? "About your age, I'd guess," I said. A son who loves cooking, a daughter who teaches Italian.

*— to imitate the blue vault of heaven —*

We talked until well into the afternoon, moving on to Maison Berthaud and coffee and wicked marzipan cakes. I mentioned Frank in passing, and she countered by saying there wasn't anyone in her life at the moment, and how on earth had I sustained a relationship for so long? Luckily we were not drawn into that, because she suddenly realised the time. Her current temping job involved occasional evenings. A large computer firm. Working for one of the Managing Directors. Taking minutes for boring meetings.

*Music —*

That evening Frank was later than usual. A drink with regional reps. No, he'd grabbed something to eat. We watched the late news, and then he noticed my copy of Hamlet on the table. As usual, he didn't ask a direct question, and as usual, I offered up information.

"I'm thinking of reviving my Hamlet," I said, just to see what effect that would have.

He looked startled.

*I shall sing to my own accompaniment on the lute —*

"But aren't you —" he began — "A bit old?" I helped. "There's always makeup."

"None of us is as young as we used to be," he said shortly, gathering up a pile of papers and inventing a yawn.

A few years ago I would have retorted with some quip about us both looking young for ever, he would have smiled, I would have ruffled his remaining hair, kissed him in the hollow of his neck. Now there was an invisible barrier round him. I knew that if I found his warmth and tried to touch him and talk, he would brush me off with excuses about work to prepare for the following day.

*Eighty trumpeters wearing cloth of gold and purple —*

He went upstairs and I phoned Lucy.

*Twenty drummers —*

"Good timing," she said. "I was about to ring you. There's a touring production of Hamlet coming to London next week. All-Italian, all-female cast. Shall we go?"

"But I don't understand Italian," I said.

"Come on," she said. "You know the story. Anyway, the Players Scene is in English, apparently. Is Tuesday okay?"

*Four lutes. I shall sing to the accompaniment of my lute.*

On Tuesday evening, the atmosphere outside the theatre was amazing. Italian families greeted, kissed, hugged, touched and talked across each other.

*At the back of the stage, a golden goddess of fortune seated on her throne —*

Inside, we ate a pre-dinner snack; Tuscan red wine, a marble floor, shiny and elegant, pasta and rucola salad. Lucy seemed a bit pre-occupied.

*— bearing a sceptre adorned with a dolphin —*

"Is anything wrong?" I asked. "Not exactly," she said — I leaned over the table.

"He's asked you out?" She looked up, surprise in her eyes. "I have an instinct for these things," I said. "Sub-text. That's one reason why I'm such a good actress. Has your boss asked you out?"

*Two rope dancers will descend on opposite sides of the stage.*

"Well, not exactly asked me out," she said, hesitantly. "We had dinner once —"

"After working late?" She nodded. "And once we went to a sort of late-night reception thing."

"After working late?"

"After working late."

We both laughed, and then the bell went. "He's married, of course," Lucy said, as we took our seats.

"Of course," I said, as the lights dimmed and the music began. Toccata and fugue. Bach. A little later than the setting of "Hamlet", but why not, I thought, as I eased into the familiar, intricate music.

*A golden ball will appear and then melt into the air.*

The play was marvellous; vibrant, energetic. The audience loved it, laughing with pleasure at seeing actresses playing soldiers, rapt at Hamlet, a slight, blonde young woman, evincing intellect and emotion.

*The four Virtues are revealed: Faith, Hope, Charity and Lust.*

Then came the Players Scene. Toccata and fugue again. In the dumb show, where poison is poured into the ear of the king, provoking Claudius's admission of guilt, the actress in the role of the Player King looked straight at the audience. Her eyes seemed to find me. Beside me, Lucy shifted in her seat.

*When I was five, I was betrothed to Francesco. He was fourteen.*

And of course, at that moment, I knew. At the end of the play, Lucy and I left the auditorium while the stamping and clapping and "bravos" were still ringing out.

*I love Francesco and he loves me.*

We drove away in silence, and then I spoke. "An odd coincidence," I said.

"How do you mean?" she asked.

"Oh, come on, Lucy. You know what I mean. That you should come to interview me when you're having an affair with my husband."

She ignored the last bit.

*I know that Francesco has a mistress —*

"He suggested it, you know," she said. I braked, and we were almost thrown forward. I steered into the kerb and stopped. I turned to Lucy.

"What do you mean, he suggested it? He made the first move, you mean? He took you to a hotel? What?"

"I mean," she said, "he suggested that I should come and talk to you about Hamlet."

For a moment I couldn't believe that I was hearing right. It was so — blatant, stupid — I didn't know what. Then a bitter light dawned.

"Of course he did," I said. "He wants my approval."

*— and children —*

"What?" Lucy almost shouted. "Why should he want you to approve of my playing Hamlet?"

At that moment I believed that Lucy was stupid and manipulative. Then I remembered our intelligent conversations.

"He wants me to approve of you," I said gently, "so that he doesn't feel guilty."

"I don't follow that," she said.

"Well," I said, "he probably feels guilty that he's having an affair with you —"

Lucy interrupted me. "I didn't say he was having an affair with me —."

"No," I answered. "You didn't. But my guess is that you have slept together, and that in some kind of convoluted way he thinks that if you and I meet and get on, then I will be less suspicious, and he will feel somehow absolved of the fact that he is lying to me. I know it doesn't seem to make sense; I think it's what you might call male logic."

"He suggested that I should come and see you because I wanted to play Hamlet and you had —"

"He wanted to let himself off the hook," I said.

"But how?" asked Lucy. "Why should he want me to meet you?"

"God knows," I answered. "Maybe having decided to have affairs, he needs to think of me as his mother rather than his lover."

"Has he had other affairs?"

"Oh, probably." As I said it, I realised that I almost believed it.

*(I have always loved Francesco)*

I drove Lucy home in silence. I was very aware that she hadn't admitted that she had slept with Frank. Nor, however, had she denied it. I wanted to know, of course, but I also couldn't be bothered to pursue the point.

I arrived back at her house. She turned to me. "I'm leaving the job," she said. I nodded. There wasn't really anything for me to say. She got out of the car. She closed the car door and walked up the steps to her front door. I drove away.

*For the play, I wore a black velvet robe —*

When I got in, Frank was watching tele. I flung my bag down.

"You've been having affairs," I said.

*— a gold collar studded with diamonds —*

He looked up. I repeated the word: "Affairs."

"Isabella," he said.

*Isabella —*

"I don't know what you're talking about."

*La prima donna del mondo*

"I thought I came first —" I began.

*The first lady in the world.*

"Hit and run, that's you," I shouted. I flung my bag across the room. "Toccata e fuga, hit and run."

*They say I have the magic of Orpheus.*

"You're hysterical, Isabella," he said. He came up to me and put his hands on my shoulders. "You need treatment."

*My name is Isabella.*

I pulled myself away from him and ran upstairs. For the first time ever, we slept in separate rooms.

*Isabella d'Este.*

Reader, I shot him. Well, I would have done if I had been living in the Renaissance and had the protection of the Pope. Toccata e fuga. Hit and run.

*At the end of the show —*

But this is the 1990s. That night in bed, I couldn't sleep. I rehearsed various scenarios in my head. We cried and held each other; he confessed his mid-life crisis, his affairs, his need to have power and be adored, his fear of dying. I talked about my fear of being overtaken by younger actresses. Together we faced growing older, and entered a new and fruitful phase of life, based on our deep love and shared history, a new partnership. Pigs might fly.

*Shepherds wearing rams' heads fight each other.*

In fact, I moved out. The following day, after he had gone to work, I packed a small suitcase, went to the bank, carefully drew out half the money in our joint account, and got a train to Broadstairs. Here I stayed in a bed and breakfast for a couple of weeks, and began looking at advertisements for jobs. I began working in a small Arts Centre, and have found a niche working on Shakespeare plays with primary school children. I tell the stories and play all the parts.

I have had no contact with Frank and no contact with Lucy, though I read the rave reviews of her performance as Hamlet. My son and daughter, after their initial shock, enjoy coming to the seaside for windblown holiday weekends.

I am not sure whether this constitutes a happy ending to the story, but then who is to say whether "Hamlet" has a happy ending? Or whether Isabella d'Este was happy?

*Isabella... Isabella...*

# Musical Chairs

*Curled up in the snow. Firm and soft. Warm inside and warm outside. His body cradled in a white shape, his head curled comfortably on a slightly higher mound, his arms folded across his chest, hands bunched inside his gloves, legs curled upwards, his knees touching his elbows. The watery sun glazes the snow, a translucent, bluish light seen through the curtains of his eyelids. His whole body is smiling. This, he thinks, is the garden of Eden. He could float forever, weightless, free. No need to know whether he is in the air or on the ground, indoors or outside, in day or night, in silence or sound. Moving or still. Asleep or awake. Voices or silence. F sharp or B flat. Whatever they are. Pussycats or monkeys. A bubble of laughter tingles. Did he say these things out loud? It doesn't matter. No-one can hear.*

At first they thought I was dead. The doctor didn't want to loosen my clothes in the sub-zero temperatures. Speed was of the essence.

They worked swiftly and silently, their boots scrunching in the snow, small grunts, tiny clouds of steam, warm air as they breathed out, evaporating as it cooled rapidly. They laid me on a stretcher. A nod from the doctor and I was winched up to the helicopter. The rescue team strapped on their skis, ready to go back down the mountain. Under the top sprinkling of new snow, one of them found an empty whisky bottle. Lucky devil, they smiled, this probably kept him alive.

*Arcs of criss-cross space, filaments, trajectories stringing through the pure air. The sounds are clean and white and sweet and have distance between them, as though they are being played by an invisible orchestra spread out in a gigantic semi-circle, across an arctic continent as far as the eye can see, some of the players below the curve of the earth's horizon. How on earth can the conductor see them all? As he strains to see, the players appear, scattered, wearing their prescription black and white. The white of the men's shirts and the women's blouses is different from the white of the snow, faint timbres, pink, lilac, peach, blue, as if reflecting the vibrancy of the living skin, the bare faces and hands, none of them affected by the cold.*

In the helicopter, the first thing I said, even before I opened my eyes was: "That Sibelius is a fucking great composer." Someone laughed out loud in relieved hysteria.

*Now he sees the conductor wielding the baton, long hair swirling, head nodding and shaking in rhythm, long, flowing hair catching the light as it swirls and sways. Delicate hands hold the baton firmly. The conductor's back is towards him. Who is it? He runs through the names of all the conductors he knows. None of them have quite that combination of firmness and delicacy. Who could it be? There is something about the angle of the head, something —— no. Impossible. It is no-one he knows.*

In the hospital I was crazy with impatience. "I'm filming next week. I've got a thousand things to do. When can I go home?" They soothed me, muttered things about a hairline fracture to my collarbone, pulled the sheets more tightly round me, tucked them in, kept the bed neat and contained me in a white cocoon far more dangerous than the snow. The newspapers covered the story with appropriate headlines: "Film director saved from avalanche." I didn't see them. I didn't care.

*The conductor disappears. Now there are just the musicians, all playing. Then the sound goes. He can see them bowing and fingering and blowing and plucking, but he cannot hear anything. Then, suddenly, the conductor is there, facing him. She is smiling. Jane stands there before him, slim and exquisite in tie and tails. Smiling.*

Be careful, they said. No coughing, no laughing, no vigorous exercise. If you promise to look after yourself, you can go home.

*She raises her arms, the baton held loosely in her right hand. She begins to conduct. She is facing him.*

*She is conducting him. Common time, she says, this is common time. Four in a bar. Four what in a bar? Come, now, you know what four in a bar is. Four men getting pissed out of their minds in the pub at the end of the road while I have to get the kids to bed and get ready for the concert. He screams. She turns away from him, back to the orchestra, raises her arms and leads them sweetly into the Adagio. Damn her.*

Back in London there were endless meetings. The composer's widow, retained as an advisor on his music, knowledgeable to a fault about his intentions. After all, hadn't she written it all out for him in her own fair hand, so much more legible than his? Had he not entrusted her with the task of protecting his traditional airs and modern graces from any inappropriate interpretation after his death?

*He screams again. The orchestra disappears. The vast expanse of snow is smooth and untouched. A white sheet crumpled smooth over a double bed. A white sheet crumpled and curled round two small bodies, their limbs flung easily and carelessly over his. God, what a flat. One large room painted white, a kitchen area at one end, barely room for a table and chairs, certainly no room even for an armchair. The older two staying Saturday nights with him. Not the baby, of course. There they are, the three of them, cuddled under the blankets in that double bed. He fought Jane against their coming to stay, and ten minutes after they arrive, he knows he doesn't want them to go away again. Ten minutes after he has*

110

*delivered them back to Jane, he flings himself back*
*into his work.*

The project took off like a dream. I'd wanted to make a film about the composer for years, and when he died suddenly, I thought I'd blown it. His widow, whom I knew slightly, told me about the last symphony. She offered to play it through on the piano to me. I refused. No, I said, I'll hear it when they rehearse it. What do you mean, she asked? I've got this marvellous idea, I said. I'll raise money for a film, a co-production, with German television, with American television, with Japanese television, and I will make a film about his life, the film I always wanted to make, and the world premiere of this posthumous symphony will be on film. How about it? Crazy, eh? But not as crazy as I was for the whole of last year, sweet-talking the men with the money, with no more aesthetic sense than a rubbish bag, into believing they were a cross between James Agee and Dilys Powell. I was exhausted by the end of it. But successful. As always.

*Their last holiday together in Scotland. Their last family holiday. Caught the car-train, arrived in Perth, spent the first night in a bed-and-breakfast in Blairgowrie. The town bleak and desperate, full of bleak men. The local canning factory shut down six months before. On the window of the careers' office, a notice pleaded: "Does your drinking cause you and your family problems? We don't ask you to give up your drinking, just come and talk it over over a cup of coffee."*

111

*Supper that evening was reconstituted Scotch broth darkened with an Oxo cube, salmon surrounded by salad and swamped with chips, a bottle of Heinz salad cream. Afters was thawed strawberries, watery, with cheesecake. The sound of a Hammond organ drifted into the dining room.*

*Later, the kids asleep, down in the bar, a nightcap whisky, and the lady of the house sits at the organ, her back to the room, the colour telly on with the sound turned down. She plays "Beautiful Dreamer" and "Home on the Range". Next morning, as they drive away, a lone piper stands on a hill, playing "Scotland the Brave", the tone lifting the landscape, the tune drifting high above the fumes and the drizzle.*

When I know what I want to make a film about, I find the form. I puzzle and puzzle, and one day it all begins to come clear. I hate films of concerts, the audience sitting there, the players shiny, stuffed; I don't mind when I am at the concerts myself, one of the audience, glorying in the excitement of the living music. I just can't stand seeing it on film.

So I puzzled away for a long time about the best way to take responsibility for the world premiere of a symphony by a Scottish composer whose work had not been sufficiently appreciated during his lifetime. No concert, I thought. Then how to play the music, how should the music be seen to be played for the first time in a way which would last forever, because it would be recorded on film?

Rehearsals. That was the answer. It was obvious. I would film all the rehearsals, then I would intersperse the biographical stuff with the rehearsals for the posthumous symphony. There would be no need to hear the whole work complete, because by the end of the film, the complete work would have been heard.

The composer's wife was intrigued, and prepared to go with it.

I love rehearsals, people turning up in any old clothes, carrying sandwiches and bottles of water, the conductor doing his own performance, with a mixture of esoteric musical jokes, sarcastic jabs, putting his whole body into the music, shaping it, guiding it, attacking it, moulding the hydra into one unit, and then standing back and letting the orchestra simply flow with what they have learned.

*Jane has brought two scores with her. He doesn't say anything, but she knows that he doesn't like her working when they are on holiday. Learn to read music, she'd say, and then I can explain what I'm doing. I'll teach you. No need, he'd answer. He hates those lines and squiggles and splodges.*

What instruments do you play, they asked me on chat shows? I don't play anything, I'd answer. I'm musically illiterate. How can you make films about music and musicians, then, they asked? Easy, I'd say. You don't have to be a soldier to make films about war. What is music, they'd ask? I can't tell you, I'd answer. It's beyond words. It has nothing to do with anything else in my life. It has nothing to do with the words with which I try to make sense of the world and try to control my life. Music can be inappropriate to an occasion, it can be played out of tune, it can be boring, but it has the supreme virtue of being beyond words, and that is why I like it. It sits in your head like an advertising jingle, or the latest pop chart hit or a fragment from a string quartet. It inhabits you. Sort of like the music of the spheres, they'd ask? Yes, I'd say, you could say that.

*Jane doesn't understand. He doesn't know how to explain it. Sooner or later people always want your soul. Music simply has it without asking. He gives it freely, voluntarily, willingly. He is Faust and the music is his Mephistopheles. The deal is simple. His soul in exchange for the time it takes to play a piece of music. Unlimited borrowing, with no fines for anything overdue. The best sort of investment, better than people. People always want your soul, sooner or later. But how can you love music and not want to understand how it is made, Jane insists.*

We spent the main part of the holiday in the hotel complex at Aviemore, ideal for the kids and handy for walking. The baby bounced on my back or Jane's, and the other two alternately moaned or looked forward to the treats of lunchtime miles away from everywhere, with a view totally lost on them.

Sprigs of heather plucked from the summit of summer Cairn Gorm. On each stem, a full nine bells of pale purple flower, each bell pouting to a narrow opening, the hood protecting the delicate interior from the mist. Walking through the drizzle, carrying sprigs of heather. Small, spiky leaves, dark green, littering the stalk to its strong base.

One day we took a chairlift up to the middle station of Cairn Gorm, the kids screaming with excitement and fear as we floated above the burn, thrilled to bits as the chairs slowly came down to earth. Two parallel lines of rocks marked the path to the summit. Signs warned climbers to beware of sudden mists. I wondered what it would look like in the snow.

*At three he remembers clutching a toy music box. It played "Baa baa black sheep". The first hymn he ever heard in school was "Oh God, Our Help in Ages Past". In later years "The Lord is my Shepherd" (Crimond) sang him through the summer holidays, tune and descant. Buddy Holly rode by his side on a bicycle through university and early married life. Mozart made friends with the late Beethoven quartets. Then Jane took up her music again, after the birth of their second child.*

We didn't talk much on holiday. Mostly we were sorting out the logistics of the day, dealing with kids, meals, clothes, outings. Some evenings, when we faced each other across the dinner table, having sorted out the arrangements for the following day, the little silences interrupted us. How was it that two people who were so closely related, who never lost the desire to touch each other, even after they had stopped touching each other; how was it that we couldn't make it work any more?

We knew the obvious problems: Jane hated my world, the world of high-powered hustlers, a world peopled with acquaintances who moved on with the end of each project, a world whose excitement I loved. And yet she liked my films. Always. And wanted me to make them, and urged me to continue making them. In turn, I could bask in the sounds of the music, but could not stand the musicians; their disinterest in what they were playing astounded me. And every time Jane opened a score, I froze in the face of these signs which I couldn't interpret and which were second nature to her.

*He can't take his eyes off the ground. He knows that if he looks up, he will be whirled away, the sky will swirl him into its vortex, the evil in him dragging him round and round, swinging his body by the head, gashing his flesh on the rocks, ripping his skin away.*

We went to Loch Ness to look for the monster. We had tea in Inverness. We watched the salmon leaping in Pitlochry. We climbed the steep path to Arthur's Seat in Edinburgh. I held the kids' hands tightly, but I was more scared than they were. I couldn't take my eyes off the ground.

*He remembers a joke told at a ceilidh. On the day of judgement, all the men in the world get together to go to heaven, and when they get up there, St Peter says, all the hen-pecked husbands go to one side, and all the non-hen-pecked husbands go to the other. So there's a huge queue of hen-pecked husbands, and only one chap on the other side. So St Peter says to the one man, you must be a brave chap, and the man*

*says, Oh, no, I'm standing here because my missus
telled me tae.*

We loved the ceilidh; the piano so sharp it was
almost flat on the next semi-tone up, Jane told me.
The kids clapped and stamped. The baby snored.
The next morning we drove back to London. I took
in the luggage while Jane made tea. When the kids
were in bed, we sat opposite each other in the
kitchen we'd planned, with the clock ticking quietly. We looked at each other. It was beyond words,
this. I said, I'm going. Yes, said Jane, if you hadn't
said it, I would have. So I packed some things and
went to stay in a hotel. I was a danger on the roads
that evening, driving my car, crying and playing
Dusty Springfield. I wanted her, I wanted me, I
wanted us.

*He knows exactly how he is going to do the film.
First, the biographical stuff shot on location in
Scotland. Then the rehearsals filmed in London,
then the wonderful editing process, when everything
would fall into place. A week's holiday before it all
starts; a skiing holiday.*

*On the last day of the holiday, he catches sight of
a headline on the Arts page of an English newspa-
per: "Conductor sacked," it says. The orchestra lined
up to play in the film had risen as one and rebelled
against their conductor. Discontents which had been
rippling for years finally came to a head. Crisis. The
orchestra's work had to continue.*

*Underneath the main headline was a subtitle:
"First Woman Conductor", and there she was, slim*

*and exquisite in her tails, holding her baton delicately, her arms raised. Jane. Smiling.*

When I got back from holiday, I dumped my luggage in the flat and took a train straight to Scotland. I bought a bottle of whisky. I hired a car and drove to Cairn Gorm. The sun was bright on the bluish-white snow. I took the chairlift up to the middle. My head was empty. Nothing. No song, no music, nothing. I got out of the chairlift. Signs warned climbers about sudden mists. I took the top off the bottle and drank as I walked. When I found a comfortable spot, sheltered from the wind, I sat down and finished the whisky. I was almost asleep before I got to the end. I was cosy, comfortable. I slid down in the snow, curled up and waited for the music of the spheres.

*At first they thought he was dead. He was still, he didn't seem to be breathing. Then, when they realised he was alive, they worked swiftly and silently. When he was on the stretcher and being winched up to the helicopter, the rescue team strapped on their skis, ready to go back down the mountain. One of them nearly fell over something half-buried in the top sprinkling of new snow. Lucky devil, he said, this probably kept him alive. He's going to have one hell of a hangover.*

When I got home from the hospital, there was only one thing to do. I phoned Jane. Did she know what a bastard I was on the set? She didn't doubt it, she said. Under the gentle, artistic exterior, I was as big a shit as anyone else. Yes, but did she mind? Of course she bloody minded, but I had to remember that she was a professional and this was a job. If I treated her badly, she would give as good as she got. Do we hate each other, I asked. I shouldn't think so, she said. We just can't live together. We got in each other's way. So can we be friends, I asked? Oh, I shouldn't think so, she said. But there's no reason why we can't work together. The music will be wonderful. The orchestra is great.

*When the committees nominate the film for its various awards, they always choose the same extract: in it an orchestra, the players dressed in their customary black and white, play the entire symphony, spread out in a gigantic semi-circle, scattered as far as the eye can see, some of the players below the curve of the earth's horizon. The white of the men's shirts and the women's blouses picks up timbres different from those of the snowy landscape: pink, lilac, peach, blue. Before them stands their conductor, slim, in tie and tails, her baton moving precisely, her long flowing hair catching the light as her head dips and sways.*

Just before the film's premiere, I bought myself a book on the rudiments of music. I can't understand a word of it.

# Rick

**harmony** n. State of being harmonious; agreeable effect of apt arrangement of parts; (Mus.) (study of) combination of simultaneous notes to form chords (cf MELODY); sweet or melodious sounds (*harmony of the spheres)*

\*\*\*

In a tiny village somewhere in West Africa, at one time colonised by the French, Rick arrives, with his back pack, his Californian check shirt, his duffle bag, his descant and treble recorders, hell-bent on getting out of mad, loud America.

He grew up in the sunshine and the sand of surfing fraternity, always a little thin, a little pale, a little too sensitive, enjoying the sea and the waves, but only first thing in the morning or at sunset, when the beefies had gone in, having found their girl for the night.

The only son of parents who never planned to have children, who lulled themselves into a quiet life in which they found peace and comfort in each other's presence. He worked as a telephone repair man, lucky to have his own van, and used to a silent working day, apart from the polite exchanges with customers. She was a school teacher, of children up to eight years old, a stranger to anything apart from polite adult conversation in the staffroom or in the supermarket. Both of them only children of only children.

When they met, they discovered a fierce catharsis in telling each other about their childhoods, the secret games they had played, rejected or teased by other children. There, in their solitary rooms, they discovered they had read the same books, invented the same worlds, built forests out of discarded matchsticks, made a broken train set stand for the first railroad in the States, used their dolls and teddy bears as inventors, magicians, gods.

Ethel and Carson found that, despite being of opposite sexes, they imagined things in the same way. Both had acquired self-sufficiencies, since that was easier than learning to communicate. So he had taught himself to cook and she had taught herself the intricacies of electricity. Their love of silence was important to both of them, they agreed. They speculated on the nature of silence, and agreed that they did not know what it was. They didn't know if it was happy or unhappy, just that it *was*, and that it was important.

Ethel and Carson met at college, where he was majoring in electrical engineering and she was majoring in English. They married straight after graduation, Ethel a blushing virgin bride, Carson proud and resplendent in a new suit he had saved up to buy from his vacation job sticking labels on decanters of Californian wine.

For the first few years of their marriage, they lived in one room and saved. Their spare time was largely spent working out budgets, drawing up lists of furniture, poring over plain colour charts, thinking about wooden floors and planning for their first real home together.

They bought a tumbledown shack near the sea, south of Santa Monica, and then all their spare time was spent sawing and hammering and mixing and painting. The sea was their swimming pool, and they didn't bother with the movies because there was always so much work to do on the house, and so much satisfaction to be got in doing the work.

They agreed that they would not contemplate having children until they had a real home of their own, and then, when they had their home, there was always something to finish off, something else to fix, and before you knew it, some twenty years had passed and the time was still not right to talk about having children. Finally, even the thought of the thought of children was no longer there in their minds. Until, that is, Ethel's trusty diaphragm, scrupulously used and regularly checked, let them down.

When she missed two periods, she began to think the menopause was starting early, so she went to her doctor. The doctor asked her all sorts of questions and then examined her. The doctor was young, and she told her gently that she was pretty sure she was pregnant. Ethel sat up from the examining couch in surprise and said she couldn't possibly be.

Yes, she had put on a bit of weight recently, and she was feeling a bit hungrier and lazier than usual, but she didn't feel sick, and she used her diaphragm regularly, she couldn't possibly be pregnant. Why, they hadn't decided yet whether they wanted to have children. It must be the menopause; actually, she wouldn't really mind, because she hated having her periods — the doctor interrupted this unaccustomed fluency, and suggested a urine test just to make sure. She suggested another appointment next week. Ethel was perfectly happy to come in next week; she was repapering the hall and it would give her time to get it done.

The following week Ethel again sat opposite the blue-eyed doctor, who told her that the test was positive, and Ethel was definitely pregnant. Ethel didn't know what to say, so she said nothing. The doctor asked her about it, and she heard herself asking whether it was safe to have a baby at her age. It's a little risky, said the doctor, but you're fit and well, and with care, there should be no problem at all. Ethel thought it made it sound as though she just had a sore throat. I know it's probably a bit of a shock, said the doctor. Ethel nodded. What does your husband think, asked the doctor, would he like a child — would you like a child? Suddenly Ethel's voice was strong and clear. Oh, yes, she said. I am sure he — I am sure I — we would. Good, said the doctor, getting up from her desk. Next time you come to see me, do bring your husband.

Ethel gathered her coat, smiled at the doctor and said thank you and went out. Behind her, the doctor looked at the closing door and then for some reason found tears welling up in her eyes, and she put her head down on her arms and wept. Then she blew her nose on a Kleenex and buzzed her receptionist to send in the next patient.

At home Ethel and Carson took the diaphragm and held it up to the light, stretching the rubber gently. Nothing. No light shining through a pin hole. There, said Ethel, it must have been magic, and they laughed and Carson took the diaphragm and ripped it apart and threw it in the garbage can and they laughed again. They were used to planning, and preparing for the baby came easily: they made lists of colours and cribs, buggies and baby clothes, but they never discussed how they felt about having a baby.

Ethel was terrified of the pain, and Carson was scared at the idea of a wild, wordless creature suddenly appearing into the lives they had managed to order through the practical use of words. He and Ethel were both afraid they might not love the child, and each was afraid to confess this to the other.

They were both taken by surprise at the joy of the birth, at its concentration, at the wordlessness of the labour and its achievement. They were unprepared for the rush of pure joy they felt when they first saw the little, red, screwed-up face of their son. They both burst out laughing and the baby burst out crying and there was a wordless happiness.

Rick grew up in this totally loving, but largely silent household. He did not speak in whole sentences until he went to school at the age of five. Doctors thought he might be backward, or deaf, and every time he was put through a series of tests, he emerged smiling, always showing great intelligence and quickness, as long as he was not expected to talk a lot. His IQ was high and there was nothing wrong with his larynx. It was only a matter of time.

In the early days of their marriage Ethel and Carson had picked up an old piano at an auction, thinking it might be nice to learn to play. But they had been so busy that the piano remained, tuned and polished, in one corner of their living room, facing the sea. When Rick began to crawl and climb, he discovered the piano stool, and one day Ethel opened the lid of the instrument, just to show him how to make sounds. From then on the piano was never closed. He soon picked out nursery rhymes with his fat little fingers, and from then on Ethel had no worry about leaving him alone in the room. He played happily at the piano for hours. Ethel could hear him from everywhere in the house, so she knew he was safe. It never occurred to her or Carson to give him piano lessons. The sounds he made were his own, and they loved them for that.

Once at school, he began to speak sentences. He learned to read and write. He played tambourines and drums, and one day the teacher brought in a handful of Japanese plastic recorders. The children pounced on them, blowing a cacophony of sound, harsh, shrill, wild. Rick took one and went into a corner, where he put his fingers over the holes, and then blowing into the mouthpiece gently at first, and then more firmly as he felt the way his breath produced the sound. Then he found that by using his tongue against the part that was in his mouth, he could define the beginnings and ends of the notes, and he began experimenting, controlling the column of air with his tongue and his breathing, making a full, rounded sound, quite different from that of any of the other children. At the end of the day he cried when the teacher tried to take the recorder away from him, and she relented and let him take it home.

From then on, Rick abandoned the piano and spent long hours with the recorder, playing the music he was given in school, but mostly playing alone in his room, a sweet, solitary sound. Soon his teacher brought some treble recorders in, and Rick began playing that too. He played in the school orchestra, and was given solos to play. Ethel and Carson enjoyed what they heard, and Rick never asked for anything more than he had.

And so the years passed. In Rick's older school, there was no recorder orchestra, so he continued to play alone, in his room. He was quiet and unobtrusive, made no friends, and no enemies. He went on to college, and one day he got a message to go and see his tutor.

The tutor's face was solemn. There had been a fire. Rick's parents — both of them — the tutor watched Rick's face carefully. He did not like to have to break news like this. Rick voiced it for him. Were they in the fire? The tutor nodded. Did they — ? I'm afraid so, said the tutor. Rick did not cry. He went home, arranged the funerals, received the sympathies of people who were all unsure about what to say to this strange, unmoving young man.

There was insurance, but Rick did not want to rebuild the house. He sold the land, put the money into the bank and then prepared to return to college. As he was packing to go, he realised he did not want to go back. He realised that the past, present and future no longer moved in a straight line, and so he applied to the Peace Corps. He wanted to get as far away as possible from America.

To West Africa he went, after a language course, the relevant jabs and a course in tropical agriculture. When he first arrived in the village, the children followed him round, chanting jeering French phrases, mindlessly learned from their parents and grandparents, hangovers from the time when the white French had ruled in that part of Africa.

Rick had been in the village for a week when he first played his recorder. One evening, he was sitting in the hut which had been given to him, at the edge of all the other houses, and he took out his treble recorder, and played a few notes, runs, scales, an occasional arpeggio. He became aware of noises outside the hut, voices whispering agitatedly. He stopped playing and went outside.

A group of villagers were clustered outside the hut, and as Rick emerged, one of the leaders stepped forward. They were all angry and worried because they did not like music in the village at night, in case their ancestors were disturbed by the music. Rick immediately apologised, and said he had not been told about that before he came, and of course he would not play music again at night. The villagers had a strong sense of hospitality, and added that since the music was white music, perhaps their ancestors would not mind. They would ask.

That night Rick dreamed he was playing his treble by the fire, when his mother and father came towards him out of the fire, took the recorder away from him and threw it into the flames.

The next day, the elders came to Rick and said that they had asked their ancestors, and their ancestors had said that all music at night disturbed them, but they did not mind white music during the day. Rick nodded and said he would not play at night.

The agricultural project progressed. Rick grew lean and strong, at ease with the villagers, respected by them, conversing with them in their language. The children stopped jeering at him in pidgin French. Sometimes, on village holidays, he would play his recorders for them, imitating their music and playing his own, and they would listen or dance. But he played very little. Back in America, the most important time for his playing was the evening, when he was away from other people, when he had regained the pleasure of his own company.

Now that he could not play after sunset, he returned to his hut at night, took the recorders out of their plastic cases, kept them by him through the evening, and put them away again when he went to sleep. It was nearly as good as playing. As he looked at the instruments, he could hear the music in his head, and that was nearly as good as playing.

Rick's one-year tour of duty was nearly at an end. Harvests had been reaped and the villagers versed in new, more efficient ways of farming. The village was too remote to benefit from the use of massive machinery, and Rick's presence served to show how they could make better use of the resources they already had. From their initial suspicion at the motives of help from a faraway, rich country, they had come to like Rick, and see him for his helpfulness, rather than for anything uncomfortably political.

The elders asked Rick if they could prepare a farewell feast for him, a way of saying thank you. Rick was delighted. He felt at home here and he did not want to go. But he knew also that he could not stay.

Meetings were held to discuss how the feast should be organised. This was a new occasion; their existing rituals would have to be adapted. Much arguing went on late into the night, keeping Rick awake.

The week leading up to the feast and Rick's departure, there was a diversion. A herd of rogue elephants had been seen some way away. Messages had come from other villages, warning of the animals' fearlessness, their seemingly wanton sense of destructiveness. They trampled crops, they attacked children and animals. Then news about the animals died down, and attention switched to the impending feast.

On the appointed morning, Rick, as the guest of honour, was decked out in flowers, ivory, beads and carvings. He apologised for having nothing to give the village in return, and they laughed at him, and one of them sang a song about how much he had taught them, and Rick was delighted. The villagers laughed and said they had worked on the song and kept it a secret. It was their main present, they said, one he would not be able to take away with him, like an ivory necklace, but one which would stay in his memory. Rick went and got his recorders and asked the villagers to sing the song again. He played with them, counterpointing and harmonising, and playing his own thank-you without words. The villagers applauded, and sent Rick to rest in preparation for the feast that evening.

In the centre of the village was a huge fire: meat was roasting, fruits and vegetables were prepared. Everyone brought something, a choice delicacy, a dance, a jump, a kiss from a little child. The village brew was eagerly drunk, and everything became pleasantly hazy and soft and Rick was both sad and happy, sad to be going, happy to carry his memories with him.

For a while no-one noticed a heavy rustle on the outskirts of the village, and then, as the evening wore on, one of the younger men came rushing into the centre with the message that the troupe of elephants had been sighted on the edge of the forest. They looked as if they were heading toward the village.

No-one was sure what to do. Because of the revelry, the lookouts had not been so keen at their watch, and it was too late to distract the elephants and draw them away. Then Rick stood up, a little drunk, a little shaky, and offered a suggestion. He wanted to play something, he didn't know why, but he thought his ancestors were telling him to. He knew that the village ancestors did not like music at night — but if he spoke to them, and explained that he was leaving — perhaps they would not mind, just this once. The villagers were not sure, but Rick was confident, and this was the Rick they trusted, the man who had brought new ways to them, and had not deprived them of their old ways. This was an exceptional time, they thought, so why not.

Rick took his recorders and, playing now on the treble, now on the descant, and now on both together, he made an extraordinary music. The village was still. As they listened, watching Rick by the fire, playing so smoothly that it sounded like a harmony of many instruments, sounds below sounds and above sounds, as they listened and watched, two figures emerged from the fire, a man and a woman, in shadow, dark and glowing. The villagers began singing their own songs to Rick's music, and the man and woman took burning branches and carried them away, like bright beacons, down the path which led out of the village, towards the forest.

There was a thunder of sound, like a storm breaking, like the sound of a gigantic earthquake, the sound of a herd of elephants in retreat. The villagers sang on and Rick continued to play. The thunder gradually faded, and with it the singing and the playing faded. Gradually a soft silence took over, a sad silence, such as no-one was used to hearing in a place where there was always sound.

The fire was very low. In silence everyone dispersed and went to sleep.

In the cold of the early morning, Rick prepared to leave. The villagers clustered round, saying final goodbyes. One of the lookouts reported seeing the elephants many miles away, heading in the opposite direction.

A Land Rover was coming to take Rick to the nearest airport, two hundred miles away. Rick packed and walked round the village for the last time, stopping by the dark smouldering embers of last night's fire. By the black and grey embers he found two melted and twisted pieces of plastic, one about the size of a treble recorder, one the size of a descant recorder. They were cold by now. He picked them up and put them in his bag. One of the elders saw him. Do you think I disturbed your ancestors last night, asked Rick. Oh, yes, said the elder. Music always disturbs them at night. Didn't you see them come out of the fire?

Yes, I did, said Rick. They reminded me of people I once knew. Of course, said the elder, ancestors always remind you of someone you once knew. I think, added the elder, that you will be glad to get back to a place where you can play music at night. Perhaps, said Rick. Perhaps.

# Via Angelica

The Via Angelica leads from the valley up to the Roman town. (*Dearest.*) The Via Angelica is a wide, cool, brick corridor, with buildings on both sides, and an arched roof. It is steep enough to need steps, deep, shallow steps, which constantly speak of ascent or descent. Down this hill the condemned were led in the Middle Ages, led to execution down in the valley, away from sight or sound of the town. *(My dearest one.)* As they were led, in chains, down the steps, they passed three chapels let into the side of the rock, on the right and on the left. At each chapel they stopped and the priest prayed for the salvation of their souls.

*My darling, I have a song in my heart.*

I pass the Via Angelica every day, on my way to the Bar Cantina for breakfast.

*The song came to me this morning.*

I sit on the terrace, overlooking the valley. Today I am unusually hungry. I order a salad. I dip coarse white bread into a pool of greeny-yellow olive oil, sprinkle it with salt crystals from a small dish. The salt hits my palate, sweet and sharp, abrasive and soothing. With it I drink tea, black, hot in the heat.

*It is the song with which Eurydice laments the loss of her lover, Orpheus.*

The bread and olive oil are like cake. I am very hungry. I order and eat a hot yellow duck egg omelette, the bright yellow as dazzling as the sun already poised above the walls of the cathedral on the opposite promontory. I am in heaven.

*If everything continues to go so well, I will be able to fly out and join you on Saturday.*

After my omelette, I walk along and down the Via Fiorentina, a wide, winding road. I hug the sides of the buildings, snuggling the shadows around me as much as possible. Ten seconds walking in this burning sun makes me feel as if hell has arrived on earth.

When I reach the convent, a long, two-storey building, I turn into the half-open black, wrought-iron gate, onto gravel, between eucalyptus bushes. Windows are open, and the sounds of loud, passionate young voices singing the opening chorus of the opera spill out into the hot air.

*Only the end is left. I can't decide. Will Orpheus be torn to pieces by the Furies, as he was at the end of Monteverdi's opera? Or will he be taken up to heaven by Apollo?*

I round a corner, and a blast of cold air comes from a barred cellar window. The chill is sudden, shocking. My right foot turns on a loose stone. My balance is righted in a second, but I feel a tug just above my ankle. I find myself limping slightly. I am not in pain. I just cannot put my full weight on my foot.

*On the other hand, Orpheus and Eurydice could live happily ever after. I just can't decide.*

I reach my room. It leads off a paved stone courtyard, weeds and wild rosemary growing between the fat stones. I push open the high wooden folding door. The gloom is cool and welcoming by contrast with the heavy, burning air outside. The smell of rosemary fills the vaulted space. On the table, by a vase of yellow valley flowers, is a letter.

*I miss you.*

I storm into Pietro's room, waving the letter. What's this, I demand. The man with the jet-black pony-tail looks up from his computer.

I scrunch up the piece of paper in my hand and fling it across the room. It lands squarely in the middle of the straw-plaited waste bin. Pietro nods in approval. A good eye, he says. A good eye and a good ear. I ignore the compliment. I am furious. But the singers are not ready. Pietro shrugs. He is the composer. He is the conductor. He is your husband. He can arrive when he wants.

*I can't wait to see you.*

When I arrived here, a week ago, I found Pietro intriguing. A man of indeterminate age, somewhere between twenty-five and forty-five, black, shining hair pulled back in a pony tail, strong shoulders, bare arms below his black T-shirt, a small, tight sway from the hips as he walked. Later, I saw that the hair was somehow just a little too black, blue, almost, in hue. I caught him one morning, peering into the mirror he carried in his small black bag, looking for tell-tale signs of grey.

*Let me tell you the story as it now runs. The first Act is familiar: Orpheus and Eurydice meet, fall in love and marry. Simple.*

Pietro's chivalric codes were rusty, helpless, invo-luntary. He insisted on opening doors, allowing me to precede him, carrying my piles of music for me whenever we met in the narrow streets or in the cor-ridors, even trying to carry my handbag. It has taken a week for him to realise that chivalry and courtesy are not the same thing. He has begun to learn my English ways. I still allow him to open doors for me and to hold my chair when we sit down in a restaurant. There chivalry ends. I carry my own music, my own attache case.

*In Act Two, Eurydice is picking flowers with her friends. A snake bites her on the ankle. She dies, and is carried away into the underworld.*

Pietro gets up from his chair. Please, he says, sit down. I make us some coffee. I shake my head. I am

138

late for rehearsal, I say. I must go. I leave his office and climb, my ankle twinging, to the top of the building.

The rehearsal room looks out over the brown and green valley, the cathedral visible from one of the windows. Here, with only the sky to eavesdrop, I take the student singers through the music. Note-bashing, it is called in musicianly circles, but in fact it is a labour of familiarisation; singing the music over and over again, so that eventually the voices will move from memory, and the sounds can soar without concern.

*In Act Three, Orpheus travels to the underworld, to beg for Eurydice's release. He cannot live without her. He cannot sing, he cannot play, he cannot compose or improvise without her presence near him.*

I play the piano with the students, leaping in at any moment in the intricate harmony to sing a missing note, hearing everything, guiding them. I don't call this singing. I am marking the pitches of the music with my voice, that is all. I do not sing any more. Now I coach the students.

In this small, Italian hilltop town, an annual summer school meets to rehearse a newly commissioned opera. This year it is a modern treatment of a well-known story: Orpheus and Eurydice have been set to music by Peri, Monteverdi, Gluck and countless others. This time the composer is my husband. Pietro is the director of the school. I have arrived a week early, to put the students through their musical paces, while my husband finishes the opera.

*Orpheus needs Eurydice's silence, her willing love, in order to free his own voice.*

After rehearsal, we all go to the Bar Cantina. We sit on the terrace, perched high on the rock, so that you feel you are tipping over, flying down into the tree-tops as easily as the tiny sparrows, the uccellini, which peck at the brioche crumbs on the balustrade.

*In Act Four, Eurydice is released from the under-world, to return home with Orpheus.*

The young women students, with their bare shoulders, slippy thin straps on their camisole tops, tight trousers, sweat pants, their tanned skin shiny with evaporating sweat, their underarms shaved smooth, hug each other, sip early evening wine, swig continuously from large bottles of mineral water to keep their voices oiled. Here they shriek and laugh and chatter in an Italian far too fast for me to follow. They drown the sparrows' chatter.

*There is a condition: that on their journey back from the underworld, Orpheus must not look round at Eurydice.*

My husband and I met as students on just one of these courses. We were rehearsing Monteverdi's "Orfeo". I was singing the part of Eurydice. He was conducting. He fell in love with my voice, he told me.

*Finally, my darling, there is Act Five.*

140

That evening, I sit at dinner in the Hotel Miracolo. I have hardly spoken all day, except in rehearsal. I eat my way through prosciutto con melone, a penne pasta with some sort of tomato sauce, the name of which I did not catch. Then pollo con insalata mista, and then out of sheer greed, a tiramisu, shared with Pietro and four greedy, noisy students. Finally, though by now it is nearly eleven at night and even the stars are yawning, I drink a bitingly intense espresso coffee. Pietro watches me.

*Orpheus agrees to the condition. He and Eurydice begin their ascent from Hades.*

When I get up to go, Pietro begins to rise from his chair. I shake my head, and I leave the room.

*Orpheus walks ahead. Eurydice follows.*

Later that night, I am suddenly woken by a tiny, waspish scooter racing past, the cobbles magnifying the engine's raucous whine. Mosquitoes have dive-bombed my left hand. The lower knuckle on my ring finger is swollen. I try to pull off my wedding ring, and fail. There are three bites on my left wrist, just above the line where I wear my watch.

*Will Orpheus look back?*

On the inner part of my right upper arm, a bite spreads in a fierce invasion, the inner part of my right upper arm where Pietro kissed me.

*Will Orpheus trust his love and resist the temptation to look back?*

It was on my second day here. I was in the rehearsal room, playing through Act One of my husband's opera on the piano. Pietro must have been listening at the door for a while. When I stopped, he applauded, walked towards me, bowed, took my right hand and kissed it. Your voice is beautiful, he said. I laughed. How do you know, I asked? Because you were singing, he said gently. I had not been aware that I was singing. He sat beside me, and again I played, and this time, consciously I sang. At the end, he took my hand again, turned it over, palm upwards, and swiftly, lightly, bent to kiss the soft skin of my inner, upper arm.

*Orpheus cannot keep to his promise. He turns, looks back and Eurydice slips away, back to the under-world.*

Pietro has not touched me since.

*What does Orpheus do?*

I lean out of window to cool my hot arms, and on the other side of the valley I see the entrance to the Via Angelica, dark, secretive. The cathedral clock strikes five.

*Will he continue to charm the rocks and stones and trees with his music?*

I dress, grab a jacket and go out, walking along the silent street, heralded only by a dog which barks half-heartedly as I pass. My ankle is still tender. The sky is lightening, and ahead, under a street light, the owner of the Bar Cantina is opening his shutters.

*Will Orpheus be torn apart by the Furies? Or will he be carried up to heaven by Apollo?*

Pietro was right to compliment me on my ear. I have what is called perfect pitch. I can identify any note just by hearing it. Some say it is an advantage. I am not sure. Sometimes hearing too much can be as dangerous as hearing too little.

*I will have solved the puzzle by the time I see you on Saturday, my darling.*

Today is Saturday. Today is my last day here, alone, before my husband joins me and takes over his opera. It is his opera, just as my voice has been his since I met him. He never asked me to give up singing. I simply stopped.

*Dearest.*

Today, then, is my last day. I walk along the Via Fiorentina to the convent. The smells of jasmine and eucalyptus dart from the gaps between the buildings. I pass the entrance to the Via Angelica.

*My dearest one.*

143

I stop, and look down the wide, shallow steps. My eye is drawn by a shadow down at the end. A man in the shadows, standing at the bottom of the steps. It is my husband.

*My darling.*

A flock of bird shapes comes into view behind him. I see that they are not birds, but graceful young women, in slippy strappy tops, in jeans and sweatpants, flying round him, enveloping him, chattering like swallows, like uccellini. I cannot tell whether they are joyous or threatening.

*I have a song in my head.*

The man is surrounded. The flock recedes, upwards, into the sky beyond the Via Angelica. Once again the valley comes into full view, green, bright with early morning sun. Orpheus has been carried away by the Furies. I turn away, and continue to walk towards the convent, singing as I walk. I am no longer limping.

# Whose Peace

*Possessions or haunting activities are never arbitrary. They occur by invitation only.*
"Dybbuk", by Gershon Winkler *(Judaica Press)*

There's a knife under my pillow. There's an orange on my bedside table. I'm a very ordinary woman. I've lived my life and brought up my family. I've never got angry. Except sometimes with the children. It's safe to get angry with the children when they're late home in the winter, or when they get their clothes dirty when you've just put them on clean. Everyone expects you to get angry with children. No-one gets at you if you get angry with children. Even if you give them a little smack. Just a little smack.

The knife I've had for fifty-two years. My mother-in-law bought it for me. A bread knife. That was my trousseau. A bread knife and two sets of dinner plates. A *milchedicke* set and a *fleishedicke* set. I always kept a kosher kitchen. Well, up to a point I kept a kosher kitchen. You see, you should have two sets of dishes — ah, what's

145

the point. This is a *goyische* country, this isn't a place where being kosher matters to anyone, so not being kosher matters even less.

I'll tell you a joke. There are two old men sitting in a cafe and one orders a glass of tea with lemon, and the other orders just a glass of tea. So the first old man says to the waiter, "Make sure you bring it in a clean glass." So the waiter goes out and the waiter comes back carrying a tray with two glasses of tea on it, and the waiter says, "Which one of you wanted the clean glass?"

The orange, my daughter brought me. My younger daughter. Yesterday. She comes to see me a couple of times in the week maybe, she doesn't even take her coat off, she sits on a chair for maybe a minute or two, then she starts looking round, restless, then she marches round the room, then she looks at her watch, then she pretends she's just noticed the time, then she says in a very loud voice that she's got to go, then she kisses the air near my cheek and then she goes. Well.

You can't blame her. She hopes I'll die quietly, like I lived quietly. She doesn't like looking me in the eyes. Something about my eyes being a little watery now, something about the angel of death, the *malach ha mavet*, looking out of one eye and Satan looking out of the other, something in my eyes frightens her. Well.

She found me on the floor. On the kitchen floor. They weren't sure, some sort of stroke, something to do with the heart, the brain, you'd think with all their machines and lights they could tell, but no, you can't tell how serious it is going to be, we just have to wait and see. Meanwhile, she seems to be paralysed down one side, she can't co-ordinate with the other, she's lost her powers of speech, maybe she doesn't even understand us, she's better off in hospital where she can have every care and attention.

I've always had very strong lungs. A good voice and really strong lungs. So now, when I get really upset or even just a bit fed up, I scream. I haven't forgotten how to scream, they say at least she can scream, and can I scream, I tell you, they can't stop me once I start. I can go on for half an hour, till their faces are white, till their mouths are tight, but they don't dare shout at me because they know I can shout louder than any of them.

My knife is very sharp. I always kept the bread knife very sharp.

My other daughter is in America. She sends me cards. She sends me flowers with Inter-Flora. They make me sneeze. I hate flowers.

I've got sores on my back. All over my back. They're spreading round to my front. They're not bed sores. It's me. I'm oozing out of my skin. They itch. I scratch and scratch. They say, how can she have scratch marks all over her when she can't move her arms. They put cream on the sores. I scratch it off. I wonder if I smell. I hope I smell. Badly. The cream they put on the sores is very powerful, and in the long run it will probably work. But it makes the skin thinner, and then all of me, all the me you can't see, will come spilling out, all over this nice clean bed.

I was always a very proud housewife. You could eat off my floor, it was so clean. But why should anyone want to eat off a floor, when there's a clean, white tablecloth on the table?

I'll tell you a joke. In a restaurant, so a man wants to know the time, so he calls to a passing waiter and he asks him the time, so the waiter says, "You're not my table."

I don't miss being at home. I had enough of it. He didn't let me have the television up loud enough to hear. So who wants to sit watching a television with the sound turned down. Like it would be if I couldn't hear the nurses, if I was struck deaf and blind like they want me to be. They think I am watching the world with the sound turned down. I'll tell you, my senses have never been so good. I can hear everything. I can see everything. Good, eh?

He comes to see me every day. He sits, looking at me. Sometimes he pats my hand. Then he looks at me again. Sometimes my eyes are open. Sometimes I keep them shut. But I can see him anyway, so what's the difference. My daughter thinks he has — oppressed — me all these years. Long word, ha? It's her word. But what does she know. It takes two to make a — press, or whatever it is — and what the hell anyway. After a while you don't remember what you haven't had. You just nod and smile when they say, what clever children, what beautiful grandchildren, what delicious biscuits, a lovely chicken soup, how did you turn the heel on the socks.

You enjoy what you enjoy. Not everyone can have what they want. My daughter doesn't believe that. She thinks you can have whatever you want, if you decide you want it. It's your choice, she says. And look at her. She has lines round her eyes, her hair is going grey. Ah, forget it.

I can't chew properly so they give me this special liquid diet. It has all vitamins in it. It has invisible vitamins, all jumping up and down to keep me nutritious and healthy and well and strong. They aren't bothering with any therapy yet because I'm still too much of a vegetable and they want to notice a sign of life or will before they try and bring me back to real life. Good, eh? Real life.

I miss the romances a bit. Being a vegetable, of course, I can't read. So all the library books are back in the library. My "rubbish", he calls it. I like Catherine Cookson and some others, I forget which. Sometimes I like a happy ending and sometimes I like an unhappy ending. It depends.

My daughter, my educated daughter, thinks I waste my time reading these books. I made her clothes to go to university with, we worked hard to get her an education, now I educated her so far away from me, we got nothing to talk about. Except the children and how she is and whether she's earning a living, and none of that she wants to talk about. Well, the hell with her. Very simple. She doesn't want to talk, so don't talk. I'm invisible now, so I don't have to talk. I can talk any language I want. English, Yiddish, Hebrew, Polish, German. Any one I like, when I like. I don't care who's listening. I don't care if no-one is listening.

When she came yesterday, my daughter couldn't stay because she is going away for a couple of days and she's got a lot to do. To Strasbourg, she says, she thinks I'm not hearing a word, so she tells me all about it, with her back to me, so I won't hear her and I won't see her lips move, and she says she's going to Strasbourg because she believes it is right and time to demonstrate against globalisation and for peace and only women understand what peace is truly about, only women care for there to be a world for the young to grow up in, and now she really understands what politics means. She thinks she knows it all. She thinks she knows what everyone in the world is thinking. If you were well, she says, you could come with me, there are a lot of older women coming. Of course I don't say anything. I think of my knife. Under my pillow.

So she takes the orange out of her coat pocket and she puts it on the bedside table and she tells me about the last time she demonstrated against globalisation and she was up against a line of policemen with riot shields and she pushed against one, and he was just about the same age as her son, she has a son of twenty, and there was hatred in his eyes, she says. She says to me, my daughter, her hand still on the orange, she says to me, straight to me, facing me, so I can see her lips move in case I'm deaf, she says with pleasure, they faced one another with hate. This makes her happy. This she likes. Hate makes her happy. She doesn't want to talk, she just wants to hate. Well.

My daughter thinks she is doing the right thing. My daughter is sure she is doing the right thing. I can see in her eyes she is already somewhere else, she is thinking she doesn't want to be here with a mother who is a vegetable, that although she can hate the policeman, she cannot allow herself to hate me because she is afraid of me. And she is more afraid of me than she is of a riot shield, whatever that is. I don't care whatever that is.

I'll tell you a joke. Hitler is feeling a little insecure, so he calls up a fortune teller and he asks the fortune teller what's in store for him. So the fortune teller tells him that he, Hitler, will die on a Jewish holiday. So Hitler asks, which particular Jewish holiday is that going to be, so the fortune teller says to Hitler, "Any day you die will be a Jewish holiday." Well. You can imagine what happened to the fortune teller.

*She begins to peel the orange, so that the rind is in one long, delicate spiral.*

I can't move. I can't walk. I can't speak. I can't hear. I can't cook the dinner. I can't do the washing. I can't hoover. I can't wash the floor. I've never been happier in my life.

I got it all worked out. I can't move, so I can't peel an orange. I can't move, so I couldn't have put the knife into my handbag while my daughter telephoned for the ambulance. I can't move, so I couldn't have kept the knife under my mattress, which they never turn. I can't move, so I couldn't have taken the knife out from under the mattress and put it under my pillow. So.

The next person who comes into this room I'm going to kill. I don't mind who it is. I'm not fussy. It may be my daughter. It may be my husband. It may be a nurse or the lady with the tea that I never drink. I don't care. No-one will know. On this

151

knife, which I didn't wash very often, who needs to wash a bread knife often, on this knife, there are my finger-prints, my daughter's finger-prints and my husband's finger-prints. My finger-prints, who's going to notice, a vegetable can't kill, a potato doesn't rise up and fight back. So.

You want to know exactly how? I'll tell you. You take the knife — so. You put the tip of it against the person's heart — so. Or you could put it against their back, I suppose, but I can't show you that. So, against the heart. Then you press it in, very quick and sudden — you don't want anything to go wrong at the last moment. So.

*She dies.*

If you're lucky, there's even no blood. They keep the sheets lovely and white here.

# The Story of
# Esther and Vashti

\*\*\*

## ONE

After it was all over, after the celebrations and the
parties and the hamantaschen and the poppy seeds,
you heard no more. What happened to me? Did I live
happily ever after? Did I go back to Mordecai? Did I
become like so many women, no longer in the full
bloom of youth and hope (note how I avoid the word
"old"), with time on their hands, remembering the
past?

*Ad lo yod'im.*

I married out for a start. No question, Ahasuerus is
a goy. He didn't convert. Why should he. Did I even
want him to?

*Ad lo yada. He never knew whether I loved him or
not. It wasn't relevant.*

Is this why the Book of Esther is the only book in the whole damn megillah not to have any mention of God in it?

*Ad lo yada.*

It bugs me that no-one has been interested, that no-one has approached me to ask if they can write my biography, or even to do an interview with me. You save a whole nation — and are they grateful? A nachtige tug, as Eve would say. She does her man a favour and gets him a nice piece of fresh fruit (after all, an apple a day keeps the doctor away), and for that she is responsible, excuse me, for the whole of the evil in our world. I don't think.

*Echad mi yodea.*

Well, I feel I owe it to the world. After all, my life hasn't exactly been ordinary. And it gives me a chance to think a little about it. This is where the problems start. First of all, everyone already knows the story. Or thinks they do.

*Echad at lo yoda'at.*

The next problem is, what language am I writing in? I suppose I am writing in whatever language you will understand. Plus some little bits of Hebrew.

*Did I love him?*

Then there are things you will want to ask. Was

Mordecai my father? Was he my uncle, my lover, my husband, just a friend?

*Almost everything in this story may never have happened.*

So. Shushan. The word sounds good. A lovely city, especially for a holiday.

*I remember marzipan and silk.*

Shushan is a lovely city. A city with pogroms and anti-semitism.

*Of all the sacred books, the book of Esther is the only one that never mentions God.*

So anyway. There's one evening, Mordecai is so depressed that nothing I can do will cheer him up. I make him a meat loaf, mixed with a little milk and an egg to bind it (you will notice I don't keep kosher), with tiny potatoes roasted in the juices, carrots from the garden, and a fresh guava from our tree for dessert. He just picks, monosyllabic, pushes his plate away. I creak backwards and forwards trying to find him something nice to raise his spirits. He nibbles an almond macaroon. Thank you very much.

Oh, I suddenly burst out, if only I was fifty years younger, I'd go and sort the king out myself. I don't know why I'm saying this, but it does the trick. Mordecai looks at me for the first time this evening, and then suddenly we're having a three-way summit.

*Esther, Venus, Astara, sweet fragrance, spreading goodness, Esther, the river.*

There's Mordecai, God and me, round my wonderful, large kitchen table, made out of one continuous piece of oak from a huge tree which fell down in the storms just after we were married. Mordecai, bless him, sawed and polished the wood, and set it on a massive iron frame, it was so heavy. All our meals, our arguments, our families, our Pesachs, the Neighbourhood Watch meetings, even my second child, believe it or not, was born on this very table. He came so fast, I had no time to go into another room, so Mordecai delivered him right here. Within easy reach of the hot water and the towels.

*Esther.*

So I serve up some coffee and more almond macaroons, and after the usual how are yous, God comes up with a proposal. He will make me young again, if I will agree to what is necessary. And what is that, say I, and wouldn't it be better if you make Mordecai young again? After all, he has the king's ear, as it were. Mordecai is, by the way, the king's tutor in classical studies. This means Hebrew and Greek. The king gets bored quickly, but why should Mordecai care. He gets paid, and brings us whatever news there is.

*Esther, ha malka.*

The king, says God, must be seduced. By a woman. By you. What an idea! The handsome King

Ahasuerus being seduced by an alte buba like me. Listen, says God, I will make you young again. That way you can seduce him and become queen.

*Esther, the great Mother, myrtle.*

I find I am laughing. I look at Mordecai, who is looking down at the ground, playing with his beard. So then I realise. You knew about this, didn't you, I ask. Mordecai nods. So you weren't hungry at all this evening, I say, really angry now, and you made me run backwards and forwards into the larder for no reason except this reason. You were waiting for this moment. Mordecai nods again. It doesn't take a genius to see I'm pissed off, so God puts down his macaroon and he intervenes. (God IS a he, by the way. What woman would want the job?)

*Esther hamalka, sweet fragrance, spreading goodness.*

You will be young again, he says. You will be a virgin. God thinks this is going to tempt me! Mordecai is still looking at the ground. If the king finds you comely (that's the kind of language God uses — "comely"), then you may be in a position to convince him to stop persecuting the Jews.

*The morning star when other stars have gone to light the sun.*

Nail Haman once and for all, I ask? In a manner of speaking, says God, although in view of our

Christian brothers and sisters, that is an unfortunate turn of phrase.

I pour some more coffee. I am not sure what to say. I am not afraid of God. I don't believe in him, so I can't possibly be afraid of him. And because he knows I don't believe in him, he has nothing to lose either.

*Haman hates the Jews. The Jews bathe in warm water in the winter, in summer, in cold. The Jews dance. The Jews sing. They are happy. They must die, says Haman.*

Suppose, says God, two men love the same woman. Can they both marry her? I shake my head. Alright, he says, suppose two women love the same man. Same difference, I say. Exactly, he says. Let's try a more gender-neutral "suppose", I say. Suppose two ships sail forth, one needs a south wind, the other needs a north wind. Can you produce a wind which will satisfy both? Mordecai looks up.

*Ad lo yada.*

I'm convinced, he says. But Esther will be on her own. What if something happens to her? Trust me, says God. And we all burst out laughing. It's lucky God has a sense of humour. Trust in God? Do me a favour. Still. The laughter is my decision. The summit meeting is now concluded. God is tactful, and knows when it is time for him to leave. Think it over, he says. Wait a minute, I say, the king already has a queen. Watch this space, says God. And he goes.

*Esther, the precious stone, the wine in a golden cup, the sound of Shushan rustling in the river.*

In bed, cuddling, I ask Mordecai what he thinks. He shrugs and holds me tighter. It's a good idea, he says. A bit far-fetched, but that's God for you. We have no army to convince the king by force, no ambassadors who can convince the king by reason, no-one who can counteract Haman's poison. The king goes for an easy life. He lets Haman get away with murder. Literally.

*I am the dove about to enter the nest where a snake lies coiled.*

What do we have to lose, I ask. Nothing, says Mordecai. If the king doesn't like you, then we are back where we started. You come home, finished. I come home, I say, seventy years old, not a virgin any more. Win some, lose some, says Mordecai. We cuddle some more. This is a political operation. Except that I know we both have personal feelings. It's not, he adds, as if this was a suicide mission.

Actually, I say, all I can think of is how marvellous it will be to be able to walk fast, to bend down and tie my shoes, to chew apples and carrots, and to have long dark hair. You have long dark hair, he says. I mean my own long dark hair, not long dark hair which comes out of a bottle.

And we sleep. I do not dream.

*A crown made of pineapple, with almonds as jewels. Poppy seeds which stick in your teeth. The heavy scent of white lilies. I taste of silk embroidered with gold. Queen for a day at carnival.*

*** 

## TWO

Well. I woke up, someone else. Some people might go on about the smooth skin, the shining hair, the shape of the body curving out for breasts, in for waist, out again for bum and hips, a series of curves in space, unfilled by excess. But for me the real wonder was the flat stomach. The stomach, strong and firm from unthinking exercise, undisturbed by the expansions of pregnancy and childbirth. Just flat. As if there was nothing there, compared to the curves of breast and hips. My one secret vice during the whole of this story was that whenever I could, I would turn sideways, to catch a glimpse of myself in mirrors, in the sunlit water as I passed, sometimes even watching my faint shadow as I passed a sleek and shining slab of marble. Just to wallow, bask, revel in the frank flatness of a stomach innocent of its future.

The word is stomach rather than belly; the latter requires the mouth to open wider, to curl the tongue round the double "ll", to suggest fullness in its very sound. Stomach is the word, closing at the back of the palate with the clear "ch" sound. If anything was going to wow the king, it would be my flat stomach, the sexiest part of me. My virginity was in my stomach.

*Ad lo yada.*

From now on, Mordecai is energised. I must remain hidden in the house. We have to wait for the right moment What will he tell everyone? Mordecai shrugs. How the hell should he know.

*Ad lo yada. Think until you do not know the difference between good and evil.*

We hatched our story. Mordecai said I was called away, to look after an ill relative, a young cousin.

*This is the story of a woman and the secret she kept and the secret she told to save her people.*

So, to cut a long story shorter, I end up hiding for four years. Don't even try to imagine it. I can recite great chunks of the Bible by heart, even those long begetting chapters. My calligraphic skills are second to none, and I have illuminated more capital letters than you've had hot dinners. The dark sky and the moon shining into our courtyard have been witnesses to the sleekness of my arm muscles, my rippling thighs, the lightness of my step as I practise my dances to silent music, and still my flat, firm, comforting stomach.

*Esther is like the planet Venus, which in Greek is Astara.*

At night, in the dark, through the course of the moon's rising and waning, Mordecai and I walk through the silent streets for evening exercise, the flickering of the occasional candle or oil lamp marking our path. Wrapped in our cloaks, passers-by think we are a couple hurrying home.

*Sweet fragrance, spreading goodness.*

The time came. Nearly four years later. Vashti, the queen, gave birth to their first child. The king, used to the idea that money will buy anything, decides to clinch his programme of dominion over Persia with a huge celebration planned to last months. All the nearby rulers are invited — that is to say, they are commanded — to attend.

*I am the dove about to enter the nest where a snake lies coiled.*

These festivities are occasions on which, for obvious reasons, Ahasuerus displays his conquered and acquired treasures. Vessels looted from the Jewish temple, the king dressed in robes which had once belonged to the high priests in Jerusalem. For Mordecai this was a terrible desecration; for me, it was neither here nor there. I had never seen any of this apparel — being for male eyes only — but the principle of collecting such wealth has always struck me as wrong, no matter from whom it was stolen.

*The story of Esther is the story of the virtue of women, a fairy tale with a gallows as the moral.*

From the room at the top of our house, I could see the palace celebrations. The upper branches of the trees interlaced to form vaulted arches. Curtains of white, sapphire, vivid green and royal purple stretched between the trees, fastened by ropes hanging from silver beams, resting on pillars of red, green, yellow, white and glittering blue marble. I could not see the floors specially tiled with crystal and marble, framed with precious stones which glittered as the guests walked past, their long robes caressing the colours. I did not see the golden vessels from which the men drank, and I did not see the drinking cups discarded after each use, so that no cup was used more than once.

*Ad lo yada. Drink until you do not know the difference between good and evil.*

News was spreading that the king and his queen were not on such good terms. At loggerheads, you might say. Fighting like cat and dog, you might even say.

*Retribution, attrition, liberty, bounty, symmetry, idolatry, festivity, bigotry, treason.*

Like everyone, I had caught occasional glimpses of Queen Vashti, her face modestly veiled, probably sweating in the heat. Everyone said she was beautiful.

*Poetry and silver and blue and gold slinking from tree to tree.*

One night, as Mordecai and I were walking, a cloaked figure came towards us. We stepped aside to let the figure pass, and it stopped. Excuse me, it said, I am looking for the house of Mordecai the Jew. There was something in the voice, grand, commanding, at odds with the simplicity of the cloak. I squeezed Mordecai's arm. Why do you want him, he asked? The woman said softly, urgently. I am the daughter of Belshazzar, the son of King Nebuchadnezzar.

I felt Mordecai's belief through my arm. I put out my arm, and touched the woman. I whispered to Mordecai. Go home, I said, I will walk with her. Mordecai left me. I took the woman's arm, and walked with her in the other direction.

*Masks made of marzipan at carnival.*

What's a nice girl like you doing out so late at night? I asked.

She laughed.

You've just had a baby, I said.

A week ago, she said.

You shouldn't be out in the cold. You should be at home, resting.

I know, she answered.

So?

The king is giving a banquet.

So?

I have been entertaining the wives, so that if the men rise in rebellion against the king, I and my guards can hold the women hostage.

Doesn't sound too bad. You can rest, and eat and

164

chat a bit. We should all be so lucky.

That's not the problem. My husband, the king, Ahasuerus (she had such a formal way of speaking, using three times as many words as necessary), has ordered me to appear before him.

I waited.

Naked.

What?

I am so beautiful that I must be one of the treasures to be displayed before his male guests.

I have heard that you are very beautiful, I said. But a week after having a baby.

Exactly. For the first time ever, I am not sure what to do. There is no-one in the palace whom I can ask. So I have come to find a Jewish sage. Shall I go or shall I refuse?

I did not need to ask what the consequences of refusal would be.

I have already refused once, said Vashti. He has sent another request. And I shall refuse again.

So what do you want to ask Mordecai?

When Ahasuerus hears that I have refused again, he will ask the Jewish sages to pass sentence on me for disobeying his orders. I want to ask Mordecai to ask his fellow sages to remain neutral on the matter. At the very least, that will buy me some time to soothe Ahasuerus.

Why should Mordecai help you, I asked. After all, you have been like any other power behind the throne, urging your husband to maintain his hostility to the Jews when he was about to give his consent to the rebuilding of the Temple.

Vashti shrugs. I am a product of my time, she

165

says. To me the Jews are alien, different, other.

Look, I say, I don't want to get into a big argument about your role in all this. But you will have gathered that I am Jewish.

You obviously know Mordecai, says Vashti. So I presume you are Jewish. But I have no proof.

No, I say, and I have no proof that you are Vashti, the Queen.

Well, we either believe each other or we don't. I am telling you that King Ahasuerus has commanded me to appear before him and one hundred and twenty-seven princes of the realm, naked.

The princes are naked as well, I ask? Now I'm really interested.

Vashti laughs. Of course not. I am the only one who is supposed to be naked. But I would rather die and have my beauty annihilated than be admired by the lecherous eyes of such a group of men.

Look, I say, playing devil's advocate, can't you just do it? Just put your mind somewhere else, think of your baby.

I am still bleeding, she said,

Ah.

If I don't go, I will be condemned to death. Ahasuerus will ask the Jewish sages to pass sentence of death upon me.

And the Jewish sages, I said, my voice going into a sing-song rhythm, will politely decline, knowing that if we condemn you to death, as soon as Ahasuerus sobers up, he will blame us and have us executed, and if we beg him to be merciful to you, then he will accuse us of not respecting his authority, and he will have us executed. Heads he wins, tails we lose.

Execute, execute, execute.

We both laugh, but neither of us really thinks it is at all funny.

Why don't you just leave, I say? Take your baby and leave. You must have family somewhere.

Vashti looks at me in surprise. My family would send me straight back, she says.

I warm to the idea. I can help you, I say. I can show you somewhere you can hide.

She looks at me in surprise. Why should you help me, she asks? You are Jewish and I have a reputation for persecuting the Jews.

Don't ask me why. My reasons are more complicated than you can possibly understand.

So you're a philosopher as well?

Careful, I say, you're beginning to sound very Jewish. That's a compliment, by the way.

Alright, she says. I am desperate. The truth is that I don't want to die, no matter how grand a gesture that would make. Dying by execution is, after all, such a double bind. Either you recant and prostrate yourself and commend yourself to your executioner and whichever God happens to rule, and thereby lie and humiliate your principles, or you shout and scream and make a huge fuss, embarrassing yourself and providing yet more entertainment for the audience. No. I want to live. Tell me. I can pay.

I'm sure you can, I say. And you will. I draw her along the street. See that house over there, I say. The one with the lamp in the upper window.

Yes, she says.

167

You will be able to hide in that house, I say. For a while, at least.

But I am still in the city.

Exactly. The king will not think of looking for you so close to home. He will undoubtedly send soldiers everywhere, and no doubt all sorts of people will be killed in the process, just to make him feel better, but he will not look here.

But the house is in the Jewish quarter, she says.

Double exactly, I say, it is. The king will not only not look for you so close to home, but he will doubly not dream of looking for you in the Jewish quarter, anti-semite that you are.

She looks at me, not sure whether I am insulting her or simply stating a fact.

You look Jewish, I say. Well, there is so little difference in looks between the Jews and the Persians, that you could pass for Jewish. In fact, you will have to pass for Jewish.

Now she listens.

You will have to change the colour of your hair. Possibly wear a greying wig. You will have to stoop. You will be over seventy years old. You will have to study hard, learn Hebrew, and about the past of a woman called Esther, because that will be your name.

The baby, says Vashti, what about the baby?

Are you breastfeeding, I ask.

She nods. I refused to have a wet nurse. The king has not even seen the baby. She is a girl and I am breastfeeding.

I nod. Bring the baby. She will be the daughter of a distant relative, orphaned in a tragic accident in

168

another country, far away. You have brought her back here. You can still breastfeed her. No-one will see you.

Vashti is very still. I don't wait for her response.

You haven't got much choice, I say. If you go to anyone who knows you, they'll go straight to the king. Your only and best chance lies with this total stranger who is offering you a way out.

I take her back to the place where we met.

Go home, send no further message to the king, do not tell any of your women, do not bring any clothes with you. Feed the baby tomorrow night, and then when she is asleep, bind her to you and come here. Mordecai and I will meet you.

*The morning star when other stars have gone to light the sun.*

*** 

## THREE

And so it came to pass. The following night, Vashti and the baby came to our house. Long, silky dark eye-lashes on the baby's warm soft cheeks. Fists bundled to her chest in the swaddling band. Once in the safety of my room, Vashti and I saw each other for the first time. She, a dark, proud, pampered and imperious woman, softened by the way she held the baby. Me, a young woman, with a deliciously flat stomach, who had never held a baby before. She showed me how to support the baby's head. I kissed the baby and she smiled. Vashti told me that babies don't really smile until they are a few weeks old, it was wind. But I didn't care. The baby smiled. Her eyes were shut, but she smiled at me. Behind the baby's closed eyes God winked at me.

*Which of us wears the mask.*

Then I began to teach Vashti what it was like to be a woman of over seventy years old.

*Who holds the earth in their arms? Who made the waters of the sea salt? The waves with the briny aroma of wine? Who chains the sea so that it shall not overflow the land?*

\*\*\*

## FOUR

All hell broke loose. The queen had disappeared. The festivities came to an abrupt end. The nobles were sent home early. Soldiers rode to the far corners of the kingdom to look for Vashti. The king raged. His courtiers moved the most precious and priceless breakables out of his path, replacing them with the least precious so that he could vent his anger. Ranges of cheap earthenware were bought, to minimise the damage. The people in the country do not like a king who is not in control.

Then an idea comes to the king. The most beautiful woman in the kingdom, he says, give me the most beautiful woman in the kingdom. A virgin, is what he really means. A beautiful young virgin, so that he could conquer where none had been.

At breakfast, with Vashti upstairs feeding the baby, Mordecai said to me, this is it.

Mordecai is a clever man; he speaks and reads all the seventy languages of the world. A clever man, with a lot in his head. For this reason, because his knowledge was useful to the king in politics and in culture, he was given the post of chamberlain at court. Mordecai, despite his wild beard, his stoop from decades of reading and writing, his slightly awkward walk, is also in his way a diplomat and a politician. It was in his interest to prevent any uprising against the king, because, whatever his volatility and undoubted ruthlessness at times, the king was in a position to give permission for the rebuilding of the Temple. With a Temple, the Jews could begin to claim to be a nation, to feel a sense of pride in their identity, and to be accepted by other cultures. This was the argument, anyway.

For me, one temple more or less doesn't make any difference. I only want to live in a time of peace.

If the king was usurped, if he was murdered, say (I would say God forbid, but if he was murdered it would have been God's will, so there's no point saying God forbid), there would be real uproar, and as usual the Jews would be the scapegoats.

*Each maiden went in in her turn, after being purified with oil of myrrh and other sweet odours.*

So the young women collect. Each day a group appears before the king. He rejects most of them. The next day another group appears. This process

171

continues, with some young women appearing day after day until they too are rejected. Anyway, to cut to the chase, Mordecai brought me to the palace, I was recalled, chosen, bedded and then wedded. In that order. Remember, the king was seeking a virgin and though technically I was a virgin again, my memories were, shall we say, beyond my official chronological years. So I knew what to do, and when to pretend not to know what to do. And it was painless. I have God to thank for that!

*And the king loved Esther above all the women, and she obtained grace and favour more than all the virgins, so that he set the crown on her head and made her queen.*

The king settles down again. The drinking and the rages stop. Mordecai resumes his daily study sessions. I persuade the king that I am worth educating alongside him. In snatched moments, Mordecai tells me about Haman. He is jealous of Mordecai's position as chamberlain.

Haman has taken to wearing a long cloak, with the image of an idol painted on it, and demanding that everyone should bow down to him, thus bowing both to an earthly being, and to an idol. Mordecai will not bow down. Haman is constantly whining on to the king about Mordecai. The king, to do him credit, says that Mordecai is an old man and his knees simply don't work any more. I learn that the king is not exactly consistent. He wants to destroy the Jews, but he likes their culture. He needs Mordecai and he is afraid of the Jewish God. Why, don't ask me. I think it is because God has such a good line in poetry.

Haman cannot bear peace. He takes advantage of the king's absorption in his new life, and unilaterally sends out decrees to kill the Jews. Unexplained events happen. Women hanging out their washing to dry, drop dead. Men drawing water from the wells mysteriously fall in and drown. Shushan becomes a city in undercover mourning. Even the sky is overcast in a heavy grey, as if the sun and moon are mourning in sympathy.

*Who can pour sunshine into dark shadows.*

I have a dream. I am pregnant. I am standing in the desert and the king comes to me, wearing sackcloth and ashes. Suddenly a snake shoots up into the air. The sand whips up into a hurricane, and I cannot see the king. The snake is whirled up into the eye of the hurricane, spun into pieces. The sand dies down, the snake has gone, the sun is out again, the king has disappeared, and I am no longer pregnant.

*Cover my head with ashes.*

Haman announces to the city that he is having a gallows built, fifty cubits high, on which to hang Mordecai.

*A life of secrets.*

Suddenly I must be a politician, an ambassador without portfolio, a unilateral negotiator with no team to support me, no defence if anything goes wrong. I live or die by my actions, as does Mordecai, and as will the rest of the Jews in Shushan. There is no public glory in this. Only a necessary task, an action.

*Angels carry messages.*

Three days, fasting. Across the water, on the other side of Shushan, twelve thousand Jewish priests pray, trumpets in their hands, gilt scrolls of the law on their shoulders as they pray. Mordecai sits and prays in sackcloth and ashes. For three days I take my food into my room but do not eat. I see no-one. I am dust for three days. I speak to no-one. I do not spend my time in prayer like Mordecai and the other Jews of Shushan. I withdraw unto myself. I fast. Not because I believe in it, but simply because I do not want to eat. I drink only water. My stomach is flat as a shallow dish. A pulse beats when I put my hand on my stomach.

*Eli*

After three days, I rise. I bathe. My maids are glad to see me.

*Eli, eli*

I dress in silk, embroidered with gold, diamonds and pearls from Africa, a golden crown on my head, on my feet shoes of gold. The gold is so lightly and lovingly spun that there is no more weight from it than from the silk.

*Eli*

Usually I see the king only at his bidding. Today I am going to see the king, unbidden. I must pass through seven apartments to reach the king.

*Eli, eli, lama*

After three days of not eating, I am weak. I pass through the first three apartments. Everyone bows, stands aside, ushers me through the doors. No-one knows that I am unbidden. Each thinks someone else has taken the message.

*Eli*

The fourth chamber swims before me. Then, an angel stands before me and passes his hand in front of my face. I feel the sun and a cool breeze. His fingers brush my lips. I taste raspberries, and the smell of coffee makes me swallow in pleasure. The second angel cups her hands round my head, under my chin, her fingers stroking my ear lobes. I lift my head and smile.

*Eli. Ze lama.*

We walk together, an angel on each side, holding my hands. The fifth and sixth chambers float by, and then we are in the seventh chamber. As I enter, the king turns towards me. He has been sitting alone, looking out of the window. He is about to rise, annoyed at being interrupted — and then he sees me. I bow my head. Normally there is no ceremony between us. The nod of my head indicates fear, respect and, above all, difference.

The king turns back to the window. His shoulders are broad and heavy under his cloak, slightly hunched, as if he were reading, tense. The angels fly from me to the king. One puts fore- and middle fingers under the king's ear, and turns his head towards me. The other angel lifts the king's right hand and guides it to his sceptre.

The angels fly back to me, and float me to the king. Each takes one of my hands and cradles them round the king's cheeks. His beard is soft. He smiles at me. Today I will not be executed.

*Eli, eli, mi yodea*

After the angels have left us, I am not clear exactly what happened, because I am now faint with hunger and when desire is also with me, I cannot tell what is of the spirit and what is of the body.

*If I have found favour in your sight, let my life be given to me, and the life of my people.*

That night the king has a dream. He dreams that Haman approaches him with a sword in his hand. In the morning I kiss the king under his right ear.

*A fountain becomes a river of light.*

The king invites Haman and Mordecai to a banquet.

At the banquet the king engages Haman in conversation. Haman, I need your advice. How should I best show honour to a man whom I delight to honour?

Haman is delighted. He thinks the king is asking him what he wants as a birthday present. Haman's eyes and stomach look only upon themselves.

Well, array him in your own coronation garments, and place your crown upon his head. You can show him no more honour than that.

Thank you, says the king. You have a fine black horse, I believe?

Given me by your majesty.

And you have a cloak of fine, purple silk, embroidered with golden bells and pomegranates. And you have a sword and a coat of mail.

All given to me by your majesty.

The king looks into Haman's eyes. Bring Mordecai to me.

Haman is not comfortable with the apparent change of subject.

Mordecai. The Jew who attends my court.

The blood rises to Haman's face. I would rather give this man silver than bring him to you, your majesty.

Excellent, says the king, give Mordecai silver. Then bring him to me.

I would rather give him my horse than bring him to you.

Most excellent, says the king, give him your horse. And I tell you what, while you're at it, give him your cloak, your sword and your coat of mail.

177

And don't bother about bringing him to me. He can ride to me himself.

He can ride to the gallows which has been prepared for him. Fifty cubits high. Made from the wood of the thornbush. High enough to be an example to the whole of the city of Shushan. My ten sons worked on it, boasts Haman.

You are an excellent person, Haman.

Haman bows. He thinks that the king has been joking.

With such a cross, so tall, so strong, so imposing, there will be enough space for you and your ten sons to be hanged from it, says the king.

Then the king turns to me and kisses me under my left ear.

*This is no miracle. Just human deliverance.*

I won't say, pacifist that I am, that the hanging pleased me. I persuaded the king to have it done at night, in the dark. But then, at this distance of time, I wonder whether I even remember that accurately. It is possible that I may have persuaded the king to send Haman and his family out of the city, making sure they would never return.

*** 

## FIVE

*The story of Esther.*

Everyone knows what happened next. Mordecai was

given a high honour among the Jews — which was alright on paper, but left him with a lot of administrative work. While I was at the palace, he and Vashti found themselves — how shall I say — well, it is enough to say that he and Vashti very soon had a number of sons and daughters who took eagerly to pen and paper. Vashti turned out to have a mental agility and precision which she expressed not only in her excellent accounting and record-keeping, but also in some wonderful work on illuminated manuscripts. Her calligraphic skills almost matched mine. She learned to recite huge chunks of the Bible, to speak Hebrew and Greek. Her daughter was brought up just like one of the family.

*Some say the story of Esther is the story of the virtue of women.*

The king was so grateful to me and Mordecai for ridding his court of the corrupt Haman, that I had freedom of movement, and visited Mordecai and Vashti often. The four of us had dinner regularly. Ahasuerus either never recognised Vashti in her new relaxed self, or he pretended he did not recognise her. We were a strange foursome. Mordecai the Jew and Vashti the shiksa. Esther, the old woman turned young, who married out. The king who loved being off duty, surrounded by an ordinary (and not so ordinary) family.

*Perhaps even a fairy tale with a gallows as the moral.*

My children with Mordecai, already grown up, were in on the truth. To do them credit, they didn't bat an eyelid, and when they called me "Mother", everyone thought it was a big joke.

*Alone of all the sacred books, the book of Esther never mentions the name of God.*

Our Jewish community lived in reasonable harmony, and so, in a sense, I was a kind of hostage: a hostage to good fortune. I was never jealous of Vashti, because for some time, Vashti must have been living her worst nightmare: a life in secret, in disguise, passing as Jewish! And she such an antisemite in her early years! But she did love Mordecai, and cared for him tenderly. She too lived as a hostage.

Vashti was punished by having to live with the enemy, and I was sacrificed by having to live with the enemy. Punishment and sacrifice are, however, only interpretations which we put on events which saved everyone's lives.

*Vayehi biyemei Achashverosh.*

I now have a firm, if slightly rounded stomach, kept in check by regular exercise, though of course nothing like as lean and flat as the girl-stomach of my second youth.

# Yom Tov

She can hear the music from her hotel room. It clashes with the early morning TV, where an edition of *Whose Line is it Anyway?* is garnished with Hebrew subtitles. She switches the television off, and the music from outside fills the room. She checks her watch. Half an hour before the taxi is due.

The hotel receptionist tells her that there will be a *hamsin* today. Along the sea front the sun already burns beyond the shade. The air is still. She crosses the road and walks between two towering hotels, down a wide sweep of stone steps onto the beach.

At the back of a large square of concrete at the edge of the sand, are two enormous loudspeakers, belting out a medley of numbers: Israeli folk songs, Arab pop songs, the occasional Beatles track. On the square of concrete itself, people are dancing, freely, sinuously, some in couples, some alone, sometimes all in lines which join and break. This is not the Israeli folk dancing she remembers, this is something soft and sexy and deeply rhythmic. People join the dancers for a while, and then wander off. She watches, her body responding to the rhythms, her feet shifting in rhythm. She longs to join the dancers, but she doesn't know the steps, so she buys an ice cream. As the kiosk vendor gives her the change, he wishes her a "Yom tov". Have a good day. On the way back to the hotel, she passes a restaurant which lists a ham omelette on its menu.

The taxi arrives and carries her away smoothly. The music fades away behind them, an Arabic song, with an obbligato piping line, singing and sliding its notes alongside the voice.

***

The *kibbutz* now has a Macdonalds outside it, in the road's elbow, where you turn right into a wide drive. The taxi stops by a tree and a low, sprawling cactus bush, just before the houses begin. She pays the driver, and arranges for him to call back for her in an hour.

She has no idea where to go, no memory of the layout of the place. Just beyond the first two small houses is a larger building. She recognises the *heder ha'ochel*, the dining room, still there, but the simple oblong block has had extensions built out to the east and the west, rather like a simple cross-shaped Christian church. Outside the main door of the building is a noticeboard, listing the week's events: a birthday party, a *bar-* and *bat-mitzvah* celebration for twins, a meeting of the Kibbutz Council. She walks round the side of the building and peers through the windows. What was the kitchen is now an office, with computers and desks. The dining room looks as though it is no longer used for meals, no longer the hub of the *kibbutz*.

Further along the path down the left-hand side of the former dining room is the *beit yeladim*, the children's house. This now seems to be an outlying building for a series of large classrooms, a school which perhaps takes in children from the surrounding area. A bus timetable pinned onto a tree seems to confirm this.

She realises that she has been looking upwards quite a lot: the trees — of course, the trees are taller. After forty years, she thinks, what do you expect? The grass is certainly much greener now, the irrigation pipes concealed beneath the ground, no longer trailing between flower beds or along the edges of the paths.

She wanders in and out of the houses, never straying far from the old dining room, in case she loses her way. Vaguely, she is trying to find the house she lived in with her family, but her memory fails her and none of the houses looks or feels right.

The air is close, heavy and silent, except for the occasional child cycling along the quiet paths, a woman carrying a shopping bag, a small tractor breaking the silence, and distant traffic on the main road. She makes her way back to the dining room, and, listless in the weighty heat, sits down on a bench under the tree, by the taxi's tyre marks.

Beyond, over Tel Aviv, Europe and America are hidden in the swirl of the *hamsin*. Sand blows invisibly across the buildings, landing on car tops, the sky a thick, yellow-grey colour, reminiscent of London in the days before smokeless fuel cleared the air.

To one side of the bench on which she sits, is a cactus, gnarled, but still standing warningly green, the prickly pear, the *sabra*, the word for a native born Israeli.

*We used to knock the pears off the cactus with a stick, then roll them in the sand with our shoes or the stick, then pick them up with thick canvas gloves. Cut the resilient flesh sideways with a knife, and then, and only then, allow the bare, clean hand to grasp the edges of the dark pink, moist and slithery pear, peel back the skin, take the whole pear in your mouth, protected from the outer layer and sweetly eat it.*

Casually she sweeps one foot backwards and forwards across the sandy soil, scraping a shallow bowl at the side of the cactus. Her foot knocks gently against something unyielding. She bends down, scrapes away a light layer of sand and finds a *hallilit* buried in the sand. A recorder. Black wood for the head joint, a light wood for the body joint. An old soprano recorder. Carelessly and urgently, she plunges her hands into the sand to extricate it.

*One day, foraging for sugar cane, avoiding the cactuses, a snake slid between the rising tiras, the corn on the cob, shiny slim green leaves arching backwards from the central stem, the cobs proudly standing in the crook of the leafy branches, upright, cocooned from light and heat, silky brown fronds protecting the top.*

She holds the instrument finally, her hands now the colour of the ground, her fingers tingling with invisible transparent tiny spines which have mingled with the sand. It is exactly like the first recorder she was given. Ten years old, an English child, not a word of Hebrew, just a musical instrument with which to invent sounds.

*She hid, trembling in the high, soft jungle of corn plants. The snake disappeared, and as she plucked up her courage to move out of the green shelter, onto the path beside the fields, shots rang out. Before she had time to react, cry out, arms picked her up, and she was held close to a man's chest, his footsteps pounding on the dry path, along the furrows of the freshly ploughed field, his feet slipping, never losing his grasp on her, his feet sliding on the clods of the dark, fertile, watered earth.*

She remembers a prickly pear, eagerly bought in a London greengrocer's, tasting dry and dull. She remembers the recorder, unthinkingly left behind, replaced with a wooden equivalent, made in Germany, never with quite the same wayward sweet sound she remembered.

*There were more shots, but as the man ran, they seemed to recede. As he reached the edge of the field, he tripped and fell, his body still shielding her from the hard ground. Momentarily his heart skipped a beat; his close warm, sweaty heartbeat had caught its breath. Then her mother was running to meet them, her father lifted her and they ran back to the house with her, white with relief.*

She brushes the sand from the surface of the wood, takes a tissue out of her bag, spits on it, precious spit in this dry and dusty heat, and wipes the outside clean. Her fingers rest comfortably on the holes, and dance to tunes she remembers.

*The man was never mentioned, but a few days later, playing on the hilltop, in renewed relative calm, she heard other children talking about a man who had been arrested for trying to steal a Jewish child.*

*Her terror had smudged her memory; she thought she was the child, but she wasn't sure. But she was sure that he had saved her, this man. When she asked her parents, they hugged her and told her not to worry. She was safe. She must not go into the fields on her own again. Dangerous snakes, that kind of thing. The shots were not mentioned.*

She hears the sound of a rough diesel engine, putt-putt, its regular whining rhythm occasionally missing a beat. A dusty black taxi turns into the drive, and then slows. She gets up from the bench and walks towards the taxi, the *hallilit* still in her hand.

The driver opens the door for her, and she notices that there is a green prickly pear painted under the door handle. She chooses to sit in the front, beside him.

She makes conversation in her halting Hebrew. About the heat, the dust, how long will the *hamsin* last. She realises that as she gestures, she is waving the *hallilit*, still in her hand. The driver asks her what she is holding. She shows him. A dusty descant

186

recorder, the instrument she taught herself to play, which she lost when they packed up to leave the *kibbutz*. Later, in England, she replaced it with a dark brown plastic recorder. When she told people with pride that she played the recorder, they laughed, so she called it a flute, and everyone nodded, impressed. The *hallilit* became the *hallil*. The recorder became the flute. The girl became the woman.

She doesn't tell him all these things. She becomes aware that the car is slowing down, and for a moment she is scared. The road is deserted. Then he begins to speak to her in English. Do you mind if we stop? I want to look at the *hallilit*, he says.

When the car has pulled over onto the hard shoulder, he takes the instrument, rubs the sand off on his T-shirt, takes off the upper joint, places his right forefinger over the vent, and blows into the head joint. A cloud of earth sprays out. He takes a bottle of water from the glove compartment, and, opening the car door, pours the water through the head joint onto the dusty road. Then he replaces the head joint and plays a C major scale. It is a dusty and slightly muffled sound, but nevertheless almost in tune. He hands it back to her, and she plays, haltingly at first, then, as her fingers remember, the tune from a movement in one of Bach's French suites. He joins in, singing the bass line, a grounding harmony.

She stops before the repeat of the second half. This is ridiculous, she says. Why, he asks. We know the same piece of music. Do you live round here, she asks? Of course, he says. I was born here. A *sabra*, she comments. Not exactly, he says. I am an Israeli

Arab. A contradiction in terms, she suggests. He shrugs. Do you live here, in — near the *kibbutz*, she asks? Yes, he says, I lived on the *kibbutz* until a few years ago. Now I live in Tel Aviv. I run a small café, and my taxi service.

*Some time later there was an Arab labourer with a bad limp who worked in the fields and did odd jobs around the kibbutz. Nothing was ever said. One day he brought a handful of recorders for some of the children, showed them how to find some notes, and gave them some tunes written on a piece of paper.*

He has got out of the open car door to stretch, then he returns to his seat and closes the door. It is my leg, he says. I was injured many years ago and it has never healed completely. Without knowing why, she hears herself ask, were you shot? Yes, he replies. Who shot you, she asks. I don't know, he says. I saved a child one night in the *kibbutz*, and I collapsed when we got back to the *kibbutz*. When I recovered in prison, I discovered I had been shot. It could have been anyone. It could have been a fellow Arab, thinking I was an Israeli; it could have been the Israeli police. After all, he added, I am one of those despised by both sides. An Arab who has lived all his life in Israel. An Israeli Arab. A contradiction in terms.

What happened afterwards, she asks. I came out of prison after six months. I was never charged because they couldn't remember why they had arrested me in the first place. Just as well. No-one would ever have believed that an Arab would save a

Jewish child from the guns. I got a job sorting fruit. Why did you stay here, she asks. After all that had happened? This is my home, he says, looking straight at her. This is where I was born. This is where I live. He turns back to the steering wheel. Shall I take you back to your hotel now? Yes, please, she says. He starts the engine and they begin to drive again, in silence. I am sorry if I upset you just now, she says.

No, he says, you did not upset me. I married an Israeli woman, he says. We didn't marry in Israel. Here Arabs and Jews are not allowed to marry each other. We flew to Cyprus to marry. Here, of course, we are living in sin. But then, in a country full of sins, one more little sin doesn't make much difference. Both our families accept us, he says. Our children speak Hebrew and Arabic. You are the ideal family of the future, I say, trying to joke. He smiles.

When we arrive outside my hotel, he waves my money away. It was a pleasure to drive you, he says. A pleasure to hear you play. It reminded me of a child I knew once. And it reminded me of a dream I have often. In it I am chased by a Palestinian Arab sniper because he knows that I saved the life of an Israeli child. The man wants to explain why I was wrong. Because he can no longer live in his father's house. Because a snake bit him. Because he was forced to leave his home. I understand what he is saying, and yet I cannot speak to him. And when I am about to wake up, the man leaves me, playing a tune I have not heard for years — until today.

*If any of the fine, invisible spines stayed in your fin-*

*gers, the only way was with fine tweezers. You had to
hold your fingers up to the light, to catch the shine
on the spines which otherwise would embed themselves deeper into the skin when the hand brushed
against anything. Absorption. Concentration.*

The hotel lobby is cool, the fan circulating air round
the dim space. I order tea and iced water. I sit by the
window, looking out over the deserted swimming
pool. The *hallilit* is in my bag. My tea and iced water
arrive. The waiter asks me if I have had a *Yom tov*.

# Also Available in this Series

## WILD CALIFORNIA by Victoria Nelson
160 pages, 0 907123 848, £7

Victoria Nelson's stories, set in her native California, and New Zealand, link vivid natural settings with characters caught up in events not of their making. A San Francisco poet is kidnapped by the Russian Mafia; an American visiting a provincial New Zealand town is gradually caught up in her host's immersion in Maori culture; a hapless stockbroker is pursued by a woman living in an abandoned school bus; a Halloween party on a Sausalito houseboat takes on an unexpected dimension.

Victoria Nelson's previous books include a study of the supernatural grotesque, *The Secret Life of Puppets* (winner of the Modern Languages Association award for comparative literary studies). She is also the co-translator of *Letters, Drawings, and Selected Essays of Bruno Schulz* and author of a travel memoir about Hawaii. All the stories have been published in magazines, including *Raritan* and *Southwest Review*. This is Victoria Nelson's first book for Five Leaves.

# Also Available in this Series

## THE NIGHT SINGERS by Valerie Miner
160 pages, 0 907123 899, £7

Valerie Miner's stories consider the fluctuating definitions of family and friendship, with wit, compassion and literary grace, paying attention to geographical place and historical moment. In a small New England town a gay man and his lesbian friend explore varieties of sexual intimacy; a brother and sister reunite in Seattle to conduct an idiosyncratic memorial service for their father; a woman contemplates the family farm, located in the middle of contemporary San Francisco.

Valerie Miner has written ten previous books published by literary, academic and women's presses in the USA and the UK. Several of these stories have been broadcast on Radio 4, others published in *The Berkeley Fiction Review, Gargoyle* and other journals. "Miner is a writer of reach, audacity, range, uniquely important to understanding our time... She gives us the beat of everyday urban life" *Tillie Olsen* "Her exploration of the dynamics between friends is subtle, profoundly moving, and true." *Lisa Alther.* This is Valerie Miner's first book for Five Leaves.

# Also Available in this Series

## HOW DO YOU PRONOUNCE NULLIPAROUS?
by **Zoë Fairbairns**
160 pages, 0 907123 155, £7

Zoë Fairbairns' stories, set mainly in London and its more-or-less fashionable suburbs, occupy the spaces between words and actions, beliefs and realities. A 40-year-old woman who has never had children and never wanted to, revisits her decision; a little girl wonders why she attends a school run by a religion that neither she nor her parents belong to; 50-something lefties discover things that they might have preferred not to know about their pensions; a woman goes to meet her partner's new love, and tries to be friendly. The collection also includes an autobiographical piece reviewing the author's membership of a 1970s women's writing group.

Zoë Fairbairns' novels include *Benefits* (a feminist classic, re-published by Five Leaves), *Closing, Here Today, Stand We At Last, Other Names* and *Daddy's Girls*. Her short stories have appeared in many anthologies and have been broadcast on BBC Radio 4. She lives in London and works for a TV facilities company, subtitling programmes for deaf and hard-of-hearing viewers.